I0658057

Suddenly Fairies

Tess Janka

Suddenly Fairies

Editing and design by Kelly Andersson
kelly@AnderssonPublishing.com
Illustrations by Shelley Matheis
elance.com/s/quannelace

ISBN-13: 978-0692429525
ISBN-10: 0692429522

Acknowledgments

This book would not have been possible without the force-to-be-reckoned-with, Kelly Andersson. She not only made the book beautiful, inside and out, she showed remarkable patience with this first-time author. Thanks, Kel! A big thank-you to Beth Price, Julie Rhyne, and Barbara Pavlovic for being courageous beta readers! What can I say about Shelley Matheis' Milk Monster illustrations – they are her unique whimsical mix of realism and fantasy that very few artists can accomplish. And the biggest thanks of all to Milk Monster, who pushed her way into this story just like she pushed her way into my home. Thank you all for making my little story become all grown up and professional!

Chapter 1
Milk Monster

It felt as though my eyeballs were about to shoot out of their sockets from the pressure in my head. I wondered what the elderly patron of the arts would do if my eyeballs did indeed explode out of my skull and ricochet off her bosom. She ranted on, oblivious to the whitening of my face and narrowing of my eyelids, as the subdued lighting in the gallery lobby began causing a pain deep behind my eyes.

She had caught me as I was escaping to the ladies' room to take my migraine medicine. *Wouldn't you know, tonight of all nights, I'm struck blind and then held captive at my own art show?*

"I understand the seriousness of the state of the world's ecology," the narrow-faced, overly groomed woman complained. "But must all of these exhibits be so depressing?"

I caught myself before I rolled my aching eyes and made the pain worse. Instead, I made an excuse and fled to the sanctuary of the bathroom. As I passed the gallery owner, Christina Sydoor, I overheard an exasperated fellow artist whining to her. I wasn't the only one being tortured with complaints tonight.

"Who would do something like that? It's not funny! I just know it was one of the other artists here!"

The tall, thin, long-haired man loomed over the petite gallery owner. He pushed his wire-framed glasses up on his nose, looking close to tears. Chrissie shrugged and took his arm, turning him back toward the exhibition hall. "I'm sure it was just an accident. I'll keep an eye on your exhibit so that no one touches it again."

"Thank you. It's just that tonight is so important, you know. I think it was that awful Madonna GooGoo who did it! Jealous hag! And what's with that name, anyway?"

Their voices were cut off by the closing of the bathroom door as I ducked inside. Thank God no one else was there. I didn't think I could handle another confrontation until I'd had a chance to recover a bit.

The window allowed just enough light from a streetlamp outside to make the overhead lights unnecessary and I gratefully left them off. I set my purse on the sink edge and dug inside for the pill bottle. Just then a sudden bout of nausea forced me to lean over the sink until the sensation faded. I found the medicine and swallowed it – only a few more minutes and I should start to feel some relief.

This migraine was unusual in that I was normally given a visual warning before the onset of the other symptoms and I could take my pills in time to avoid them. This time, however, there had been no warning of any kind. But then, this was an especially stressful time. My work was being featured along with only three other artists so both my work and I were receiving more attention than usual. I preferred solitude to public gatherings, so art shows were not my best-liked pursuit. It was a necessary evil for an artist, so I did my best to get through them.

"Is this really worth it?" I asked my pale mirror-self. "Do I really want to spend so much time hawking my work instead of creating it?"

My mirror-self didn't answer but my squinting eyes caught a fleeting expression somewhere between despair and anger. This was one of the times I resented being on exhibit along with my artwork. The time spent courting wealthy patrons didn't seem worth the little they were spending in the declining economy.

My stomach had calmed and I was able to widen my eyes without much pain. My head still felt too big and heavy for my neck, but that was much easier to deal with than pain. I had to return to the gallery.

I stepped out of the bathroom into the back room of the gallery. My clay sculpture, "Earth Screams," backlit by small spotlights, had a few people standing around it. A depiction of the Earth as a woman with her mouth a cavernous space dotted with stalactites and stalagmites in place of teeth, it dominated the space. It was a good sign when people stopped perusing the buffet table and lingered near a piece.

The background murmur of voices made me think that Chrissie had to be very happy with the turnout. She had debuted Glyphs just over a year ago and was now starting to make the gallery's name known in the city's art circles. Judging by the number of people attending this show, she seemed to be well on her way, which was good news for me if I wanted to make a living as an artist. Speaking of which, I needed to get my butt over to those people by my artwork and try to close a sale or two.

I started across the room, smiling and waving to other artists. David Applethorn had, for the moment, ceased his hostilities toward Madonna GooGoo and was engaged in a vigorous conversation with a client as I passed his exhibit.

Movement next to one of his smaller sculptures caught my attention. The ceramic figurine of a man morphing into a tree was slowly turning to face a nearby wall.

As they moved into the glow of a display light, I spotted two humanoid males about six inches tall, dressed in tight, green, one-piece clothing and matching hats with long points that stuck straight up from their skulls. My disbelieving eyes stared at what looked like acorns dangling from the pointed hat-tops.

Their little faces were glowing with mischievousness as they heaved what was to them a heavy object out of its place.

I gaped, unable to comprehend what I was seeing; before I could say a word, a shriek stunned the busy gallery into a shocked silence. David had turned and noticed that his sculpture was facing the wall.

"You!" he shouted at Madonna GooGoo. She looked up, wide-eyed with surprise, from a conversation with an artist friend.

David stomped across the room to her display. "How dare you! How dare you move my work again?"

With a dramatic sweep of his hand, he knocked one of Madonna's apocalyptic climate paintings off the wall and stood there, hands on hips, as she stared from his face to the painting on the floor.

"You son of a bitch!" Madonna cried, and leaped toward him with her long nails slashing the air.

The bitch-fight was on. There was slapping and hair-pulling until the onlookers parted a path for Chrissie to intervene.

I was still watching the little green men. They apparently enjoyed the fight immensely, giggling and laughing at the chaos they had caused. I blinked, and they were gone. I turned to a woman standing next to me, who was watching the combatants being pulled apart.

"Did you see them?" I asked her.

She laughed. "Of course. I can't decide who I want to win the fight."

"No, no, not them. The little men who turned the sculpture and started it all."

The woman frowned. "What little men? All I saw was a big man throwing a big fit. Honey, whatever you're smoking, I want some." She laughed and turned away.

I looked back at David's sculptures but there was no movement. *It's the migraine, stupid. You always see things when you have one.*

As I had that thought, I saw colorless geometric shapes whirling in my peripheral vision, a warning sign that the medicine wasn't enough to keep the oncoming pain at bay. I had to leave, and now.

I found Chrissie helping Madonna GooGoo straighten her display. "I hate to interrupt, but Chrissie, I have to go. I'm getting a migraine, and I have to hurry home before I can't see well enough to drive."

"Oh, Odessa, I'm sorry," Chrissie said. "Your piece has been getting a lot of attention. I hate for you to miss that. But migraines are awful, I know. You go on, and don't worry. I'll email you a list of the people who want to contact you."

I hugged her gratefully. "Thanks, Chrissie. You're the best."

As I threaded my way through the people in the room, their moving forms left a blurry, colorful trail behind them. This was a new and worrying symptom of an already unusual headache.

The short drive home was uneventful but I was relieved to pull into my driveway. Once inside, I undressed and crawled into bed.

The headache blazed across my skull with fiercer than usual pain and strange visual disturbances. When I closed my eyes, swirling neon colors kaleidoscoped behind my eyelids. It scared me. *A doctor's appointment might be a good idea.* Usually when I threatened my symptoms with the doctor they went away.

After what seemed like the whole night, I peeked through slitted eyelids at the clock. I had been suffering only a couple of hours, but opening my eyes didn't result in renewed pain – a good sign that the headache was starting to abate. I knew from experience that the nausea would lessen with sleep. At least it usually did.

I rolled onto my side, closed my eyes, and sought comfort in my favorite dreamscape, the land of Faerie. I had discovered Faerie as a child; it was a magical place in my mind that I could escape to rather than listen to my parents fighting downstairs. It broke my child's heart to learn that Fairies weren't real, so I kept them alive in my heart and my head.

As I got older, Faerie became a ritual way to lull myself to sleep. I would still actively imagine exploring a fantastic landscape filled with tiny, beautiful Fairies until I drifted off. What a carefree existence it would be to live with no responsibilities, sipping sweet nectar from flowers, and dancing in the moonlight, free from all the societal rules that humans had to live by.

I had loved Fairies for as long as I could remember. I devoured books about them as both child and adult. I built a large collection of books about Fairies which I used as reference when creating Fey sculptures. My favorites were those by the author Brian Froud and the artist Amy Brown. Froud's depictions of the Fae were edgy and closer to nature, but Brown's Fae with attitude were hard to resist.

The next morning, I woke at my usual time, around 6 a.m., and walked to the bathroom, massaging my stiff neck with one hand. My head still felt three times its normal size, as if inflated with gas, and my eyesight was still just a bit off. Moving objects continued to trail colorful auras and I kept being startled by flashes of movement in my peripheral vision. If this didn't go away soon, I would definitely have to make that doctor's appointment.

The bathroom mirror was downright unkind. It reflected my short, brown-streaked-with-gray hair featuring unflattering random spikes, puffy brown eyes, and a marauding pimple on the tip of my nose. I took a quick shower.

The blow dryer tamed my wild hair, and concealer and makeup disguised my puffy eyes and pimpled nose. It seemed silly to put on makeup just to go to my water exercise class, but most of the women there could climb out of the pool and walk into a formal party if you looked at them only from the neck up.

I climbed into my figure-flattering black and white bathing suit, but the bedroom mirror was no nicer than the one in the bathroom. It showed a short, fat, 50-something woman standing there. Damn. I sighed and slipped a soft, well-worn cotton top and jeans over the bathing suit.

After breakfast, I checked my gym bag for my water shoes, and opened the front door. I jumped when a black and white form on the porch greeted me loudly. It was the tuxedo kitty that had adopted me a year ago. She had just appeared one day, a kitten, running up the driveway with her tail standing tall, and rubbing against my legs like she knew me. Since then, she had become a daily visitor.

She was here for her usual breakfast of dry cat food and milk, which I called her "milk and cookies." Since I didn't know the kitty's name, she became Milk Monster, because she was as crazy about milk as the Cookie Monster was about cookies.

Milk Monster meowed repeatedly, managing to sound pitiful and starved despite her glossy coat and bright green eyes. "There's got to be Siamese in you somewhere," I said. "You're such a nag."

With a put-upon sigh, I went back inside to fetch Her Highness's breakfast. Once Milk Monster was engrossed on the

porch with her milk and cookies, I locked the door and gave her an affectionate rub as I walked past. She arched her back, purred, and crunched all at the same time.

When I got to class there were a few women already in the water. Most were elderly and used the class as a form of socialization. They stood in the chest-deep water, moving in place to warm up and talking animatedly in small groups. Today my altered eyesight revealed each of them outlined with various colored auras. They looked and sounded like birds with their bright colors and chirping voices.

I stepped onto the first of the pool steps, grimacing at the cold water. This was the hardest part of the class. Management claimed the pool was heated, but it always felt quite cold to everyone in the class. I had to force myself, a non-swimmer, to step down from the last step into the deeper water.

Swimmers could dive in and just get the shock over with. It was always an unpleasant jolt for me as the water enveloped me up past my breasts. The upside to the cold water was that I had to keep moving in order to stay warm.

Beth, the instructor, wasn't there yet. I glanced at the clock. 7:45. I had 15 minutes to warm up before the class started. I selected my hand weights, waded to my usual place in the front line and began practicing some of the moves I had learned in previous classes. After a few minutes the water no longer felt cold and my body relaxed. I began to enjoy the feeling of the water and of being almost weightless.

Before I knew it, Beth had arrived and was plugging in her iPod to play exercise music. Most of the gossiping ladies broke out of their groups and the class formed five lines across the pool, each of us a good arm's length apart.

I watched Beth on the deck as she jogged in place. I was so envious of her slim body, black hair, and blue eyes. She looked like a dark-haired Barbie doll. She began calling out the routine while demonstrating on the deck beside the pool.

The class jumped rope, jogged in place, traveled left and right, and did the rocking horse. Then came time to leap out of the water. This was one of my favorite exercises. I loved seeing how high I could jump out of the water and challenged myself to jump higher each time.

"All right, bellybuttons out of the water!" Beth called, leaping nimbly into the air.

The class all began to jump, and out of the corner of my eye, something flashed on the woman next to me. Trying not to be obvious, I peeked at her. I hadn't seen her in class before but there were always one or two newbies checking out the class.

She was younger than anyone else in the class and she had a voluptuous figure. Her long blonde hair reached her waist and shone with a slightly green tint. *Too much chlorine in her hair*, I thought. The young woman burst up out of the water and I realized it was her green metallic bathing suit with a fish scale pattern that was sparkling in the light. As she leaped, I thought I saw a glimpse of matching green fins on her feet.

That's weird. Why is she wearing diving fins in here? Don't they make the exercises harder? You know, she kinda looks like a mermaid. The thoughts came and went quickly as Beth began a different routine of exercises. We all leaped, rocked, paddled, and jogged for 45

8

minutes, and then ended the class with some floating to cool down.

The young blonde woman was an excellent swimmer and pretty much ignored what the class was doing, choosing instead to dive and swim on her own. As we floated, I watched her as she swam hard along the rim of the entire pool, and then jumped out of the water, much like a dolphin. I noticed that no one else, including Beth, was paying any attention to her. She dove under with a wave of her fins and I lost sight of her.

Then it was back to the shower and dressing and going on with my day. Refreshed and exhilarated by the exercise, I was eager to get back to work on my latest sculpture.

I drove home and wasn't surprised to encounter Milk Monster lounging in the driveway. The cat looked up at the approaching car and then lazily got to her feet, stretched languidly, and then walked as slowly as possible out of the car's path.

Pretending to be annoyed, I fussed at the cat as she wound around my feet and then scooted into my path to lie down and roll back and forth. I rubbed her soft, furry belly and then the special place beneath her chin. Straightening, I let myself into the house. I hung my purse on a hook in the foyer, grabbed a bottle of water from the fridge, and crossed the kitchen to the glassed-in porch.

The porch had been converted into my clay studio and held a worktable, slab roller, shelves of glazes, drying shelves, and boxes of clay.

The views in two directions were of the woods behind the house. I loved working here – nature was always here to keep me company. Right now, the hardwoods were starting to lose their leaves, but the tops were still full and seemed to bask in the sunlight. I heard a hawk calling as it circled above the treetops.

I switched the radio on, preset to the local classical station, since I didn't like working to music with words – the lyrics tended to distract me. Then I unwrapped my current sculpture from its protective plastic. It was a Fairy sculpture, using a manikin torso as an armature. The wings were my biggest challenge with the piece, but I had figured out how to get them to dry flat, so now I could relax and just let my imagination take over with the construction.

As I began rolling out slabs and manipulating coils of clay into workable shapes, I kept being distracted by movement outside the windows from the corner of my eye. There was no wind blowing, yet I kept seeing leaves move in the trees or tall grasses swaying. Once or twice I thought I saw small animals moving, too quickly to focus on.

I tried to ignore it all, but then I saw Milk Monster pouncing on something in the weeds at the edge of the yard. I could see only her behind and tail, but she must have missed because she lunged toward another spot a few inches away from the first. Secretly I hoped that her prey had managed to escape. Sometimes I discover the tiny corpse of a mouse or mole left as a gift on the porch, and I hoped I wouldn't have to dispose of another one soon.

10

I continued to work, but then came the sound of squirrels dashing across the metal roof of the studio. The footsteps ran in circles, and I suddenly froze. Besides the sound of padded paws on the roof, I heard the sharp clicks of boot heels. *Since when do squirrels wear boots?*

I jumped up, dashed through the sliding glass door, and peered up at the roof, just in time to see a squirrel leap across to a low branch. It was followed by a small grey figure wearing boots, and before I could blink, both were lost in the trees.

I stared at the spot where the two had disappeared.

No, I did not see that.

"No," I said aloud. I went back inside and slid the door closed.

I'm making a Fairy, so they're on my mind.

I went back to the worktable.

I'm thinking about them so I think I see one. That was just a squirrel with two dark legs. This is just more of my vision playing tricks on me. I really should make that doctor's appointment.

I shook my head at myself and went back to my sculpture. I worked until late afternoon, then misted the sculpture with water and enclosed it tightly under plastic. I cleaned up and hung my apron before heading for the kitchen.

I started supper for myself, and while it baked I walked down the driveway to retrieve the day's mail. The alimony check had arrived on time, along with a couple of bills and the September issue of *Ceramics Monthly*.

As I walked back up the driveway, I gazed with appreciation at my home. It was a three-bedroom ranch with cedar siding painted brick red with the shutters and trim in white. A barn-shaped two-story garage matched the house. Old oaks and maples towered above the buildings, providing shade and adding to my sense of security.

I stopped walking as I looked at the house. It had always been my refuge and sanctuary, but suddenly I was feeling a bit sad. The cheerful red and white home was the scene of my loneliness. Since the divorce, I had retreated into my ceramics, rarely seeing anyone and until now, not missing human companionship.

Maybe I should get a dog.

As I approached the flower bed at the front of the house I saw Milk Monster batting at something under a bush. Suddenly the cat leapt backward, froze for a second, stared under the bush, and then sprang away with the crazed leaps and bounds common to overexcited cats.

"Oh, God, I hope it's not a snake," I said as I approached the bush. I leaned down, but couldn't see anything moving. I picked up a stick and crouched, carefully parting the leaves, poised to jump away just like Milk Monster, and looked into the shadows. No snake. In fact, there was nothing there. I dropped the stick. "Silly kitty," I murmured, and stood up.

The Human walked away. The tiny Sprite dressed in green watched from his perch in the upper branches of the leafy bush. His orange eyes shone as he pushed his lance, a stick with a thorn as its point, out of the leaves and made a slashing motion at the Human's back.

The next morning I felt much better. My stiff neck was gone and my head felt like its normal size again. My vision was almost back to normal, so I decided to put off calling the doctor.

No water exercise today; instead I would take a walk around Lake Apex. After a quick breakfast for myself and Milk Monster, I headed off to the park.

I parked the PT Cruiser in the park's main lot and then spent a few minutes stretching before I began my walk.

Lake Apex boasted a roughly oval 150-acre lake with four miles of paved trail and two miles of unpaved trail surrounding it. A city park, it offered boat rentals, picnic shelters, and fishing. I liked walking the trails here because many people were accompanied by their dogs and I enjoyed meeting both the two- and four-legged walkers.

The trail started off with a gentle rise into the woods before leveling out and leading to a wooden boardwalk that spanned the lake. Fishermen of varying ages clung to the rails, watching bobbers. I dodged their tackle boxes, drinks, rods, and oncoming pedestrians as I crossed the lake.

Sunshine glittered on the surface ripples of the water, creating patches of sparkling diamonds across the lake. A "V" of Canada geese flew overhead, honking as they landed on the far side of the lake. I followed the paved trail, walking briskly.

The great blue heron was in his usual spot in the shallows, standing statue-like and much too dignified to acknowledge the ducks that bobbed and dove and quarreled a few yards away. As I walked past them, a fly buzzed my right ear and brushed my earlobe. I kept going and a second later the fly repeated its aggressive fly-by. I swatted the air and continued walking.

Yet again the fly circled my head, but this time my flailing hand made contact with it, knocking it onto the pavement at my feet. It lay there, stunned.

"Oh my God!" I gasped, staring at the thing. *It has a face. It has a tiny, human face!* I froze, staring as the creature regained its senses, launched into the air, and flew away. I stared after it, my memory replaying black and white images from *The Fly*: the scientist's face on the housefly struggling in the spider web. I shuddered.

"Don't be ridiculous!" I hissed to myself, forcing my feet forward and resuming my walk. "That just looked like a face. It wasn't really. That was just a weird mark on its head, that's all. It just looked like a face."

I walked on, continuing to scold myself under my breath. "Remember the squirrel yesterday? You thought it was a Gnome. Now you're seeing faces on bugs. It's your imagination, and that's all. Stop being so stupid. Just because you saw a mutant fly is no reason to start imagining there are monsters in the bushes!"

Still, I was grateful when the boardwalk came into sight just ahead, which meant I was close to my car. There were still a couple of straggling fishermen hopefully casting lines into the lake. A trio of joggers ran past me, and a woman with two Jack Russell terriers stopped to let me pet them. This was how I usually experienced the park. There were no more strange sights, which reassured me that everything was normal. I was in a much happier frame of mind as I drove home from the park.

I had been putting off shopping for jeans, but an accident with a jar of glaze now made the trip a necessity. At Walnut Street Center, I parked in my usual area between Belk's and JCPenney's.

As I got out of the car, a crow perched on top of a nearby light pole began to caw. I glanced up at it and was surprised to see that it seemed to be looking right at me. Its feathers shone blue-black in the sunlight as it cocked a yellow eye at me, flapped its wings, and continued to caw.

Ravens are a sign of magic in the air, I remembered reading in one of my Faery books. I pressed the remote to lock the car and walked toward the mall. I had to pass beneath the lamppost, and for an instant I half-expected the crow to dive at me, but it stayed where it was. As I stepped up on the curb in front of the mall entrance, I realized that the harsh cawing had stopped. I glanced back – the crow was gone.

I entered the mall, my mind turning to jeans. The mall was busy for mid-week in September, so it looked like my intended grab-and-dash might not be possible. Young women, either singly or in pairs, pushed strollers the size of SUVs. Teenagers skipping school loitered in the hallways. Girls wearing tight jeans and tiny tops huddled in giggly groups. Boys in saggy jeans and oversized shirts posed in attempts to ooze machismo and impress the girls. Here and there an elderly man waited on a bench while his wife shopped nearby.

The carousel in the middle of the mall was turning and the tinkling music bounced off the tiled walls and window glass. Children and parents rode painted horses, tigers, and swans while colored lights flashed. Cinnabon was exuding the heavenly scents of cinnamon and coffee.

I dodged the slower shoppers until my way was blocked by two women with strollers. They were chatting animatedly, unaware that they were holding up the people behind them. One was blonde, the other brunette, but otherwise they looked and dressed similarly.

I slowed, annoyed, and then saw a small figure perched on the blonde's shoulders, giggling as he pushed her purse strap off her shoulder. The woman kept returning the strap, only to have the little creature push the strap back down.

I glanced wildly around at the other shoppers. No one else was reacting. *Oh my God!* I thought, my stomach sinking, *They can't see them! I'm losing my mind!*

I studied the little figure. He was male, humanoid, about eight inches in height, with green skin and clothing and shiny, translucent wings. His long, shaggy brown hair fell straight down from a brown hat shaped like a thorn.

I stopped in my tracks. The teenager behind me made an irritated grunt and stepped around. I saw another green figure sitting on her shoulder as she stalked past.

The young girl wore a tank top, her bra straps showing as was the current fad. The Fairy? Elf? Pixie? was also amusing itself by pushing her bra strap off her shoulder over and over. The girl seemed totally unaware of her mischievous passenger.

Without thinking, I caught up to her and swiped at the figure on the girl's shoulder. My hand connected and the Pixie fell from its perch but flew away before it hit the floor.

"What the hell?" yelled the girl, recoiling from me.

"I'm – I'm sorry," I stammered. "There was a – a – spider."

The girl frantically brushed at her shoulder. "Oh God! Is it gone? Is it gone?"

I assured the girl she was now spider-free. Once she calmed down, I made a beeline for my car. Jeans shopping would have to wait. Right now, all I wanted was to go home and call the doctor. It was time to report my migraine-induced hallucinations.

Chapter 2
Pillyswiggin, Gollysnuffle, and Fairy Dust

Your tests all look normal, Odessa," Dr. Tave said as she entered the exam room holding my lab paperwork. "Your sedimentation rate and urinalysis don't show any cause for your visual disturbances. Your last eye exam was normal, wasn't it?"

I nodded. "So you think it's nothing to worry about?"

Dr. Tave nodded and smiled. "I think it may be just a small amount of swelling that hasn't gone down yet from your recent migraine. I want you to set up another appointment for a week from today. If the symptoms are still persisting, which I doubt, I'll prescribe an MRI."

I grimaced.

"Don't worry, Odessa. I'm sure you're fine," Dr. Tave assured me as she opened the exam room door.

"Thanks, Dr. Tave. See you in a week."

I went to the receptionist and paid for the visit and made the follow-up appointment. I left the building and got into my car. As I put the key into the ignition, a tiny form fluttered onto the hood of my car.

My hand froze and I stared. *If I'm fine, Dr. Tave, why am I seeing a woman with butterfly wings on my car?*

The figure took flight and zig-zagged away. *I should run in and tell Dr. Tave – but she'll just say it was a butterfly. And it probably IS just a butterfly. It's the swelling, that's all.*

I forced myself to start the car and drive away. I was nervous all the way home, expecting at any moment to see something strange, but I arrived home without incident.

Gildan the Silver didn't like what the Pixie was telling him. His long, solemn face drew into a frown and he ran a narrow-fingered hand unhappily through his long white hair. The Pixie was bruised and one wing was bent, but he was otherwise unharmed from the incident with the Human.

"She saw me! She saw me and she slapped me! She tried to kill me!" the Pixie cried in a shrill voice. "She looked right at me and then she hit me! Only the grace of the Gods kept me from dying by her giant hand!"

Gildan shook his head. "Are you sure she saw you? Humans haven't been able to see us for hundreds of years."

The Pixie shook with indignation, his wings fluttering and sparkling as they caught the light in their prisms. "She saw me all right! She looked right at me! She aimed that giant hand and tried to squash me!"

"What were you doing that made her want to 'squash' you, Pillyswiggin?" Gildan pinned the pixie with the metallic silver irises of his up-slanted eyes.

The Pixie's righteous anger melted away and he looked down at the ground instead of at the leader of the Silver Company. "I was just playing with a Human. I wasn't hurting anyone."

Gildan sighed. "I thought as much. On your way, Pillyswiggin. Remember this the next time you *play* with a Human."

The Pixie flew away, his flight a bit crooked because of his injured wing, looking more like a butterfly than a Pixie.

Gildan strode into the Becharmed Forest, his brown skin and elongated limbs blending in with the oaks, pines, and thorn trees. His white hair shone yellow as patches of sunlight crossed it, as did his simple white cotton shirt and pants. The silver necklace he wore caught the sunlight as sharp needles of light.

The Becharmed Forest was not itself enchanted, but was named for the spell its wild beauty cast over those who beheld it. Most of the forest area consisted of ancient live oak trees that towered into the pure Faery air.

Low-hanging branches curved and twisted and dug into the ground among the trees' knotted above-ground roots. The bark was furrowed vertically and rough to the touch. Ball moss, Spanish moss, ferns, and mistletoe made their homes in the branches, along with yellow jessamine vines. Slender, tapered acorns littered the forest floor, some hidden by buttonbush thickets, broomsedge grasses, deerberry, and bracken ferns.

These trees were the homes of Dryads and Tree Elves, who guarded them jealously and would respond viciously if their homes were harmed. Gildan moved through the forest with impunity, for the tree spirits knew him.

The charm in the form of an oak tree on the silver chain around his neck was a talisman of his protective feelings and love of Faerie's wilderness.

The Becharmed Forest was Gildan's refuge – his place to go when hard thoughts were to be considered. Pillyswiggin had brought troubling yet exciting news. Humans weren't supposed to be able to see the Fae since they had gone separate ways; the Fae had returned to Faerie many centuries ago.

While Faerie and Earth were still connected, Faerie existed one realm apart from Earth. The Fae had been gone for so long that the ability to see them had been bred out of humanity. Humans had forgotten about their small cousins, and in doing so, had become utterly selfish. The Earth was no longer the sister of Faerie in its purity and untouched wilderness. Now it was a sad place, crowded and polluted; it had become the deranged relative hidden from view.

Gildan knew that the news of a Human with Sight, as untrue as it must be, would have to be verified before it was shared with the other leaders of Faerie. He sat on an oak root and gazed grumpily out across ToadSpit Lake. Groups of moss-dotted boulders weighted the shores, interspersed with small black willow trees, stands of bulrushes, and tall wetland grasses.

The water, running shallow here where the lake curved into a comma-shape, lapped over and around the large rocks that had fallen into the lake body. Lily pads floated on the surface of the greenish water. Even the sight of a flock of water sprites dancing on the surface in the sunshine, sparkling like gemstones, didn't cheer him.

Earth had a magic of its own that was quite different from that of the nature-based magic of Faerie. Humans had harnessed a wild power that allowed them to travel and communicate with each other, a power far beyond Gildan's ability to reason. Gods knew he had tried – but to this day he was as ignorant as he had been upon his initial visit. One experience stood out in his memory, and he still cringed a little upon recollection of it.

On one of his first visits, Gildan had been standing on the stone walk of a Human city, trying to figure out the purpose of the sky-lights. He was almost mesmerized by the red-green-yellow-red sequence, despite the pauses between colors. The pattern of the mysteriously-powered carriages with hard, non-wood wheels seemed to be controlled by the lights somehow. He heard a voice close to him, which interrupted his thoughts.

"Hello?" a woman said, standing right beside him. She was looking right at him, eye-to-eye! This was impossible – Humans couldn't see the Fae anymore!

"Hello," he responded nervously.

"Hello? Hello?" she repeated impatiently.

Not sure what she expected him to say, Gildan repeated the greeting. "Hello."

"There you are!" she said, still looking at him, but vacantly, as though he hadn't replied to her address. "I thought you'd been dropped."

Dropped? What in the name of the Gods does that mean? Gildan wondered, then answered, "No, I have not been dropped – that I know of," he added hastily, in case she thought his reply strange.

The woman laughed. "Actually, Marcy, I was just calling to find out what time I should pick Jake up from the sleepover."

First Gildan felt relieved – she was not speaking to him. His invisibility remained intact. Embarrassment followed despite the fact that he was unfamiliar with the workings of human magic. Then he became curious. How was she speaking to someone who was not right there?

Emboldened by the knowledge that she could not see him, he walked around her, inspecting her carefully. On the second orbit he noticed a small wire jutting toward her mouth. Upon reaching her other side, he saw a metal button in her ear. This was frustrating – he could see the magic objects, but he still had no idea how they worked.

"Okay, thanks, Marcy," the woman said, "I'll see you at nine." She stepped off the sidewalk into the road and walked past a series of idling carriages. Gildan watched her go, wondering how she knew it was safe to cross so closely to them and how they had known to stop before she stepped into the street.

Earth was just full of indecipherable magic, and his curiosity remained unsatisfied. He hated going to Earth.

Curled up in my favorite denim-covered armchair, I wiped my eyes and sniffled. *Dr. Tave is wrong. I know what I saw was real – but how could it be? That was a Fairy, dammit! I know it was. But Fairies*

aren't real. *Maybe Dr. Tave missed something. Maybe I have a brain tumor...*

I sat up straight. *No, I don't. If I did, I'd be seeing things all the time.*

Then I remembered the last couple of days – the "squirrel" wearing boots, the fly with a face, the Butterfly Fairy, the Pixie on the teenager's shoulder, even the woman in the pool that looked like a mermaid.

I slumped. *Shit, it's either my vision or a tumor. No matter how real they seemed, those were just hallucinations.*

I reached for a tissue but the box was empty. "Dammit!" I snapped.

With a put-upon sigh, I uncurled my legs and stood up. I walked into the bathroom and pulled a handful of toilet paper from the roll. Blotting my face, I looked into the mirror over the sink.

"I don't look any crazier than usual." I muttered, pushing my hair behind my ears.

Bzzzzzzzzzzzzzzzzzzzzz.

I looked around for the source of the buzzing sound. Then a small black figure stepped out from behind the vase of silk flowers on the bathroom counter. It looked like a tiny man wearing a tattered black overcoat. The hem, sleeves, and collar were frayed and long threads hung unevenly from them. His ragged wings hummed, making the buzzing sound.

I stared as he turned his little face up to mine. His features were flat and vaguely insectoid, and his long, tangled hair was like black threads. His eyes were as round and black as buttons, yet they managed to gleam with hostile intent.

Bzzzzzzzzzzzzzzzzzzz. "Keep talking," the little man said in a gravelly voice. "Someday you'll say something intelligent."

I drew in a breath to scream and the ugly little man grimaced. "Before you do that and deafen me, I just want you to know that talking to you is about as appealing as playing leapfrog with unicorns." Buzzzzzzzzzz.

I forgot to scream. Not only was this creature ugly, he was actually insulting. Forgetting my fear, I put my hands on my hips and glared at him. "What are you, anyway? A Fairy from Hell? What do you want?"

"You stupid Human!" the shabby creature replied, "You're proof that Humans use only about one-tenth of their brain power. In fact, with you, it's decidedly less."

"Get out of my bathroom!" I cried. "You're not real!"

"Oh, I'm real all right," he snarled. "As real as the blood about to flow from your throat."

And with that, he leapt at me.

Flailing my hands in front of me, I caught one of my fingernails on a thread hanging from the creepy little man's overcoat. As I pulled away, the thread followed, unraveling the coat. As I continued trying to ward off the attack, I realized that the entire body of the creature was unraveling. There was nothing left but his eyes, forehead, and some hair. The eyes shifted to look at me furiously, and with horror I gave one last tug. The eyes fell with a clink to the counter, and I was left with a long black thread hanging from my fingernail.

I stood rooted to the floor, staring with disbelief at the thread, half-expecting it to reform itself, but it just hung there limp and dead. Shuddering, I plucked it off, wadded it up, and threw it in the trash. I couldn't bring myself to touch the eyes, so using a piece of toilet paper, I brushed them into the trashcan. Then my knees gave out and I sat on the floor, shaking.

In the darkness outside the bathroom window, a pair of silver eyes watched Odessa sink to the floor, body trembling.

Gildan the Silver stepped away from the window and addressed the two Pixies fidgeting at his feet. "Good work, you two. The Impudent worked. You were correct, she does have the Sight."

He sighed heavily, then coughed upon inhaling Earth's thin, smelly air. When the spasm had passed, he said, "Go. Do as you were told. And remember, *she can see you.*"

The Pixies melted into the night and Gildan returned to the window. He watched the woman and almost felt sorry for her, but not sorry enough to let that change his course of action.

I sat on the bathroom floor and gazed at the wad of black thread in the trashcan. I reached out a finger and touched it lightly. "Goddamn it, that is real!" I snapped. "This is real! I'm not imagining this. This is not a tumor or a vision problem."

I jumped to my feet and hurried into my home office where my books were stored. I selected an armful of books about Fairies and took them to my denim chair and turned on the reading light. *Surely that nasty little man is based on something. He's got to be in here somewhere – and if he is, then I'll know I'm not crazy.*

I searched a couple of books but found nothing. There were plenty of Fae nasties, but none came close to Little Insult Man. The evening's excitement had given me a headache, so I decided to make some tea to see me through the rest of the book pile. Jasmine green tea would be a comfort. I set the pile of books on the floor in front of my chair and went to the kitchen.

Pillyswiggin pushed his brother Gollysniffle ahead of him. "You do it," he insisted in a whisper. "My wing still hurts." Gollysniffle went rigid. "Uh-uh! I don't have to go!"

Pillyswiggin glared with his unbruised eye, but Gollysniffle wouldn't budge. The two Pixies were behind the denim couch in the living room, between it and the dining room wall. They could hear Odessa making noises in the kitchen as she prepared her tea.

"Fine. Fine!" Pillyswiggin hissed. He pulled his thorn-shaped hat down almost over his eyes. "Just don't blame me if we get caught. I'm not used to hiding."

"You better go now," Gollysniffle breathed. "She could come back any second."

Pillyswiggin squared his shoulders, then winced as the movement jostled his injured wing. "All right, but it's your turn next time."

He took a few steps away from the couch and strode halfway across the floor. A noise from the kitchen sent him scurrying back to the nook behind the couch.

Gollysniffle rolled his eyes. "Some hero you are. You do know that Gildan's watching, don't you?"

"If you're so fobbing brave, you do it!"

"I told you already, I don't have to go."

Pillyswiggin took a deep gulp of air, ran in place for a moment, and then darted to the pile of books on the floor. Quickly, he opened the cover of the first one on the pile. Reaching into his green cotton pants, he pulled out his penis and aimed at the crack between the pages. He waited for a moment. Nothing. He strained … nothing. He glanced back at Gollysniffle, who was gesturing wildly for him to hurry.

Pillyswiggin heard liquid being poured, and strained harder. He only had a minute or two left, if that. He panicked, dancing from foot to foot. "Pilly, you swill-headed, gormless numpty, do it!" Still nothing.

Gollysniffle peeked out from behind the couch. Pilly still hadn't done it! The Human was going to be back here anytime now and they were going to get caught. He sprinted from his hiding place, yanked out his penis, and sprayed the pages of the book with Fairy dust, just as Pillyswiggin did the same.

They slammed the book closed and ran, penises wagging, as Odessa entered the living room with her jasmine tea.

I set the mug on the side table. It was my favorite mug, a Sheryl Wise original, with a cunning mouse sitting on the top of the handle. The tea was still too hot to drink. I curled up in the chair, picked up the first book from the pile of unread ones, and opened it. Glittery dust wafted up into my face, and I sneezed.

How did it get so dusty? I settled the book on my lap and began to read.

I had barely gotten through the first page when sleepiness pressed down on my eyelids. I blinked heavily and sipped my tea. It was much too soon to consider going to bed. I flipped the page. My eyes closed.

I woke up with a start. "What's the matter with me? I can't keep my eyes open."

"That is as it should be." A gentle voice said.

I looked up, saw silver eyes, and then all went dark.

Chapter 3
The First Day in Faerie

Sounds of murmuring voices woke me. I felt heavy, as if I'd been filled with lead. I opened my eyes and was horrified to see the glinting silver eyes of my nightmare looking down at me from a brown face framed by white hair. I gasped, recoiled, and the figure backed away.

"It's all right," cooed a second voice, a woman. "No one here will harm you."

The woman sitting on the bed beside me appeared to be about my age and size. She had a cheerful face with dancing brown eyes and a warm smile. Her thick, waist-length brown hair was plaited into twin braids that hung past her matronly breasts. The hand holding mine was warm and comforting.

"Are you a nurse?" I asked, though I had never seen a nurse's uniform like hers before. She wore a cream-colored apron over a gauzy blue blouse and matching skirt and a cream hat with a wide brim turned up to a point above her forehead.

The woman laughed, a low-throated purr. "I guess in a way I am. You can call me Lull."

The silver-eyed man stepped forward. "And I am Gildan the Silver, the Town Leader."

"Where am I?" I cried, sitting up and attempting to free my hand from Lull's. "Let me go!"

Lull hung onto my hand and with the other, gently pushed me back down onto the pallet. "Hush, hush, let Gildan explain."

"I'm still asleep," I said in a voice of discovery. "I'm in my chair in the living room with a book about Fairies. I'm dreaming you."

Lull squeezed my hand. "No, we're just as real as you are."

Gildan approached cautiously.

"Now, what's your name?" Lull asked. "I need something to call you so we can talk as friends."

"Odessa. Odessa Chase," I replied, watching Gildan with suspicious eyes as he drew a chair close to me and Lull.

I eyed his simple white clothing and shoulder-length white hair. A silver necklace with an oak tree charm glinted against his brown skin. Only his eyes betrayed his "otherness." It looked as though his irises had been silver-plated. That should have made him appear cold or inhuman, but his countenance, while boasting aristocracy, bore no cruelty. His energy was calm and dominant.

My heart raced and I gasped for air. "Let me go. I want to go home!"

Gildan the Silver smiled. "We are no longer in the business of stealing Humans," he said with a hint of amusement. "You can go back to Earth presently. But before you do, I must ask that you take counsel with me first."

I looked at Lull. She nodded and patted my hand. Her eyes told no lies.

"Wait a minute. 'Back to Earth?' I'm not on Earth? What are you? Are you aliens?" I began to panic again.

Lull laughed. "You're such a fearful Human. Calm yourself and Gildan will explain away your fears."

I propped myself up with my back against the wall and placed the pillow in my lap. At least now I was physically on the same level as the "aliens." That was a small comfort, but at this point any comfort was welcome.

"All right then, tell me where I am." I still didn't believe this was anything more than a dream inspired by the Fairy books.

Gildan shifted his weight in the hard wooden chair and crossed his legs. Lull winked at me and rose.

"I'll be in the kitchen for a lamb's shake. Some tea will make us all more comfortable." She disappeared into a connecting room.

"You are in the realm of Faerie, Miss Chase."

I shook my head. "That can't be. You and Lull are as big as I am. And I don't see any wings."

"Not all Good Folk are tiny and winged. We couldn't very well farm if we were only a few inches high, now could we? No, the Folk can be as small or as large as we need to be. The same holds true for wings. Not all Folk can fly, nor do we need to. We adapt to our environment, you see."

"I guess that makes sense," I admitted. "But where is Faerie? And why did you bring me here?"

"Please indulge me while I start at the beginning." Gildan settled in the chair, preparing for his explanation. "Three thousand years ago in Human time, the Folk returned home to Faerie. Until that time, we co-mingled with Humans on Earth. There were some problems, but all in all, it was a satisfactory arrangement. Then the Human population exploded and eventually it became clear to us that the Human God's will was that Humans should take over the Earth." He cocked an eye at me. "I daresay you've done quite a good job of it."

I couldn't help but smile a little. *Here I am, talking to a Fae. This is very cool, even if it is just a dream. Wait a minute – did he just mention God?*

"Wait a minute. Did you just say 'God?'" I echoed my thoughts.

"Yes, why is that a surprise? Humans have a God, don't they?"

"Some do. Probably most do," I acknowledged. "Are we talking about the Christian God here?"

"To tell the truth, I am not sure of that," Gildan admitted. "It is our common belief that our Creator made the Folk in between Humans and Angels. Perhaps the Creator is the same as your God, perhaps not. The Angels have the Heavenly Realm, we have the Faerie Realm, and you have the Earthly Realm. I would imagine that our Gods differ just as our realms do, but I cannot be sure of that."

It's really too bad that this is only a dream, I thought. *This is fascinating! I hope I remember this in the morning.*

Lull entered the room carrying a tray with cups of tea and a plate of what looked like pound cake. She bustled about, serving Gildan first and me second before she settled with her own cup.

Gildan sipped his tea and smiled. "How is it that your tea is always better than my own?" he said to Lull.

Lull grinned. "It's my secret ingredient, and don't even think about trying to pry that out of me, Gildan the Silver or not!"

He chuckled.

My own tea and cake sat untouched. I knew better than to consume anything in Faerie – the books and movies were full of warnings about that. To do so would create a permanent yearning for Faerie food. The only way to satisfy that yearning would be to – oh my God! This food really was a trick.

I'll show them I can't be so easily fooled, no matter how hungry or thirsty I get.

"You still haven't explained why you brought me here," I said, to get the conversation back on track.

Gildan looked at me over the brim of his teacup. "If you want to know the truth, it is because I do not know what to do with you."

My eyes widened. "Is that a threat?"

He laughed, almost spilling his tea. "No, no. What I mean is ..." He thought for a moment. "I believe I left off with the separation of the realms. Yes, I did. You see, when we returned home, over time you Humans lost your memories of us. As the years passed, your belief faded along with those memories, and we became stories that grew more and more fanciful with each telling. Finally you became unable to see us at all. Even now when we visit the Earthly realm, we are invisible to you."

Gildan paused as Lull re-filled his teacup. "We know that we cannot be seen, and that makes for some irresistible opportunities for mischief."

"I still don't see what any of this has to do with me," I complained. *This guy just likes the sound of his own voice.*

Gildan looked slightly irritated. He obviously wasn't used to being rushed.

"This has to do with the fact that *you* are Human, yet you can see the Folk in the Earth realm. You interfered with some random Pixie play, did you not?"

"Oh," I said, embarrassed to have missed the obvious connection.

"You are an anomaly. I brought you here so that I could speak with you about this. As Town Leader, it is my responsibility to determine whether or not your ability to See is a threat to us. Were you born with Sight?"

"No. I'm as surprised by this as you are. I've never seen anything like this before … until just recently. Oh my God, the migraine!" I sat straight up. "A few days ago I had a headache. It was the worst I've ever had, and once it went away, I began seeing – things. I don't know how or why, but I think that headache made me able to see you."

"So you are unaware of any other Humans who can See?"

I laughed. "Oh, people see ghosts and aliens, but I haven't heard of anyone truly seeing Fairies except in their imaginations. Like I'm seeing you right now."

Lull's cup clattered against the saucer. She and Gildan exchanged a look and then she looked at me.

"You haven't touched your tea or cake," she said.

"I'm – not hungry," I replied lamely, not looking at her.

Lull's merry laughter rang out once more. "I know what's wrong. Lamb's ears, it's been so long since I've watched over a Human that I'd forgotten. The poor thing thinks that if she eats or drinks anything here that she'll be bound to Faerie forever." Lull explained to Gildan, then turned to me. "That's an old Earth myth, Miss Odessa. I'm not sure how it started, but it's not true."

I glanced at the tea and cake. I was thirsty, but I still didn't trust the food – or the Fairies.

Lull clucked her tongue against the roof of her mouth. "You're going to get very hungry and thirsty if you refuse food and drink for your entire visit."

"It's all right. I'll get a Diet Coke when I wake up." I reassured her.

Lull shook her head in wonder. "You still believe you are asleep?"

I nodded. "I have to be. Otherwise, I'm totally insane."

Gildan was beside me before I saw him leave the chair. He reached out and with strong, sure fingers, pinched my earlobe. I yelped and jerked out of his grasp.

"You are wide awake and in Faerie!" He glared at me. "The pain is real, is it not?"

I stared at him as the realization settled into my brain. He must have seen something change in my face, for he stepped back to his chair, sat down, and finished his tea.

I looked at Lull and she nodded solemnly. "It's true, Miss Odessa."

My stomach turned a somersault and I clutched the pillow to my chest.

"I'm not a threat to you," I said softly, forcing my fear away. "But what will happen to me if you decide I am?"

"Happen to you? You will stay here in Faerie. However, this is a matter that must be discussed by The Silver Company before it can be settled. My opinion is only one of many."

I looked at him with dismay. "But you said I could go home!"

"If I have my way you shall, but you must be patient while we sort out this problem. "

"What problem? No one would believe me if I told them I was seeing Fairies!"

"We do not know that for sure, Miss Chase. You are exhausted. For now, take comfort in the fact that we have no intention of harming you." Gildan gestured toward Lull. "In fact, that is why you are with Lull. We have had a few Humans here before, and we have found that giving them a companion is the best way to avoid any missteps. Lull will guide you as you learn our ways during your stay with us."

I couldn't stop the tears that were sliding down my face as I gazed at him. "I'm not going home anytime soon, am I?"

He glanced from me to Lull and back. Then he shook his head. "Bureaucracy moves at a snail's pace in both of our realms, I am sorry to say."

My silent tears turned into great, braying sobs as I released my fear and sadness. Lull got up from her chair and sat next to me. After a moment, she pulled me across her ample chest and I let her hold me. I was too worn out to fight. And Lull felt good, like a mother.

Lull looked at Gildan over the top of my head as she rubbed my back soothingly and let me cry.

"You've upset her enough for one night, Good Sir."

Gildan stood. "Please believe me when I tell you that you are in no danger, Miss Chase. I will do what I can to ensure that you see your home again."

I didn't answer him. It was finally starting to sink in that this was not a dream. I could hear Lull's heart beating against my ear, feel her warm, heavy arms, and smell a gingery aroma from her apron. This was no dream.

Lull eased me down onto the mattress and tucked the pillow under my head. She drew the blanket over me. Then she took Gildan's arm and accompanied him from the room. I could hear them talking for a few minutes, and then the door opening and closing.

When Lull peeked into the room, I feigned sleep. She withdrew and I opened my eyes. I lay in a strange bed, in a foreign land, and struggled to hold onto my sanity.

On the morning of my first full day in Faerie, I awoke just after sunrise. I could hear Lull snoring gently on the bed pad across the room. I slipped on my shoes and quietly left the room without waking her.

I stepped outside the cottage and gasped. Faerie was even more beautiful than I had imagined. The cottage was constructed of stone in a circular shape. A shell of stones patterned to look like woven strands wound around it. The domed roof peaked in the center, and like an umbrella, hung over the sides to slant water away from the foundation.

From the little stone cottage on a hill I turned and looked down onto a distant cluster of wood and straw buildings nestled between ranges of hills on either side. The wood buildings were unpainted, but the straw roofs shone in the morning light.

Behind the village rolled rich farmland bordered with hedges and hills. I saw fields of grains and beyond to orchards. Meadows dotted with livestock ended in forest, the trees almost black with distance.

Woodland covered hills melted into mountains that rose into the cobalt Faery sky. Puffs of white mist were slowly rising from the hills and lay suspended so that the mountain peaks appeared to be rising out of the clouds.

This is what Earth used to be, I thought, breathing the clean, silky air. Almost without realizing it, I began to walk. I didn't approach the village, yet too shy to approach any of the residents of this strange and pastoral landscape. Instead, I followed a well-worn path toward a pleasant forest. There was a perfume in the air – I suddenly realized that I had never smelled truly fresh air before. It was delicious.

True Fall had not yet arrived here in Faerie, I noted, as I passed a meadow still rich with blooming flowers. Blue and white asters were showcased by towering black-eyed susans and purple sage. Showy stonecrop, with its pink star-shaped petals and tiny white cup-like blossoms, peeked over the grass.

A buzzing sound caught my ear. At first I thought a late-season honeybee was simply making a round of the flowers, but then I saw a Sprite about three inches tall, using a hatpin for a sword as he battled a honeybee for access to a black-eyed Susan. His armor delighted me – walnut shells protected his torso and an acorn cap served as a helmet. He balanced himself like a fencer and poked at the bee as it lumbered past him, almost losing his precarious balance on the flower's center.

The honeybee seemed enormous in comparison with the Sprite. Although the Sprite was adorable in his nut-shell armor, with only a hatpin for a weapon, he seemed outmatched. I hurried over and shooed the bee away.

"You ruined it! How can I win the tournament now?" The Sprite began jumping up and down in fury. "You meddlesome, worm-sucking, eye-offending whoresdaughter!" he screamed in a high-pitched warble.

Only then did I notice the other Sprites, similarly armored, who had taken possession of other flowers. I had walked into a contest. While I was distracted, the Sprite reached out and jabbed the hatpin into my knee. "Get out of here, you giant puttock!"

"Ouch!" I jumped back, more startled than hurt. "All right, all right, I'm sorry. I didn't mean to interfere."

He was still slinging insults after me as I walked away. Here I thought I was doing a good deed and instead I had infuriated him. I couldn't help but feel a little foolish.

Guess I'd better not act so fast. Everything is different here, even if it is pretty.

Birds sang from their treetop perches and sunlight dappled the underbrush and footpath. Lights glinted ahead and proved to be a shallow stream, making merry music as it trickled over its pebbled bed from a lake. I picked my way past the tall grass and willows lining the lake's edge and sat on one of the boulders grouped at the water's edge.

"I can't believe I'm really here," I murmured, dipping my hand into the cool water.

Minnows darted in and out of the nooks between rocks. The sun warmed my shoulders.

"This is real. I'm really here," I said, though still not quite convinced.

As beautiful as all this was, fear nibbled at my insides. I just didn't feel "normal." My emotions felt blunted and shortened. Was I in shock or was this an effect of being in Faerie? Would my emotions come back in full force and reduce me to a quivering mass of flesh? Or would I be content to stay in Faerie forever, never feeling homesick for my Earthly home?

Also, Gildan had never really answered my question about what would happen if I were judged a danger to the Fae. I believed him when he said they wouldn't hurt me, so the only alternative was spending the rest of my life here.

Would that really be so bad, a traitorous voice asked inside my head as I gazed at the lovely lake. *What do you have back home to keep you there? You live alone, you work alone, you're divorced, your parents are dead, and you have few friends. Just what is it that you can't give up?*

A neon blue dragonfly flashed by and perched on a tall reed near me. My attention was diverted from the dragonfly by movement near some lily pads suspended on the water. My eyes widened as a trio of water nymphs lifted themselves out of the water and onto the broad, floating leaves.

They were tiny, perfectly formed female humanoids. Their silvery skin sparkled like fish scales. They had seaweed-like green hair that framed their faces. Large, round fish-like eyes dominated their little faces. They were close enough that I could even see their elongated fingernails flashing as they gestured and laughed.

I sat still, hardly daring to breathe as the water sprites chased each other across the lily pads. The three nymphs skidded to a sudden stop and peered into the water. One pointed, and then all three dove into the water without making a splash.

I was disappointed to have had such a short time to watch them. But moments later, the nymphs bobbed to the surface, carrying a struggling frog onto the shore. The frog fought but was unable to escape because the nymphs had buried their long fingernails deep into its flesh.

As I watched, horrified, the beautiful nymphs tore the still-living frog into pieces. One of the nymphs lifted a dismembered frog leg to its open mouth and I saw pointed, sharp teeth rip into the flesh.

A shadow fell over me; startled, I almost fell into the water.

"Shame on you, Miss Odessa. You frightened me to death!" Lull scolded. "Come back with me and let's have breakfast. Surely you're hungry enough by now to trust that my food is safe for you to eat."

I smiled at her. "I trust you. I'm just not sure I want breakfast after seeing that."

I pointed to the water nymphs still eating the frog. One was buried to the waist in the frog's belly.

"That's just their way," Lull said, taking my hand and guiding me off the boulder. "You shouldn't be straying. There haven't been Humans here for hundreds of years. We don't want you running into any of the Good Folk without me there. Seeing you might frighten them and cause – consequences."

I almost laughed. The Fae frightened of me? From what I had seen, I was the one who should be frightened.

Sitting at Lull's kitchen table, I looked around while she bustled about serving breakfast. It was a small, cozy room with curtainless round windows and a hardwood floor. The table and chairs were handcarved with intricate designs of vines and flowers on the table legs and slats of the chairs. Instead of running water, a handpump supplied cold water into a pail in the dry-sink. Lull cooked on a wood-burning stove; the kitchen was warm from the stove's heat.

Despite my earlier assurances that I trusted Lull's cooking, I warily eyed the cup of tea and bowl of oatmeal that sat in front of me. Lull added a plate of sliced bread and a small crock of butter to the table. I was so hungry and thirsty and the food looked and smelled so good – it was torture to just sit and look at it.

My instincts remained at war with my intellect as Lull sat down across from me and slathered butter and jam onto a slice of thick, crusty bread that was still steaming, ignoring my plight.

I watched her and my stomach growled.

But it's Faerie food and everything you've ever read says over and over that it's a trick to bind you to Faerie, my mind insisted.

But how long will you be here? How long can you go without food and water?

It's a trick.

Lull hasn't lied yet. You trust her.

As if on cue, Lull tucked into her oatmeal. It had been generously laced with milk and honey. I picked up my spoon. Hesitated. Lull bit into her hot bread and the aroma wafted toward me.

I scooped a small bite of oatmeal onto the spoon and tried to sniff it inconspicuously as I brought it to my mouth. It smelled like – oatmeal. I stuck the tip of my tongue out and barely touched the mound of cereal. It tasted like – oatmeal.

"Lamb's behind!" Lull cried, startling me so badly I dropped my spoon into my lap. "Eat your porridge, Miss Odessa. It is not enchanted!"

Embarrassed, I retrieved the spoon and ate my oatmeal along with two slices of bread. It was heavenly.

Between bites of hot buttered bread, I learned that Gildan owned the property but lived in town and that Lull operated the small farm here. This area of Faerie was called Agrarian Lea, since most of the inhabitants were farmers. Everyone grew their own food and sold the overage at market.

Lull cultivated root vegetables and raised cattle for milk and butter, chickens for eggs, and pigs for butcher. A small herb garden supplemented her pantry.

As we cleaned the breakfast dishes, Lull said, "When we're finished here, we'll hook up the wagon and go to market. I need a few things."

This was both exciting and troubling news to me. I was nervous about meeting the other residents of Agrarian Lea, but I was also curious.

Chapter 4
The Faerie Market

ull led me outside to a barn behind her cottage. The foundation was an elongated triangle of wooden pole supports with tightly woven straw covering the frame. Two wooden stalls held miniature horses, who chuffed the air when they caught scent of Lull's approach.

Lull stroked their foreheads and reached into an apron pocket.

"This is Zebedee," she said as she fed a brown and white paint horse a carrot.

"And this is Nur." Lull gave the white horse a carrot and patted its neck.

I was delighted when both horses accepted a piece of carrot from my hand. They were perfectly proportioned, yet barely reached our hips, and Lull and I were only five feet tall.

"They like you," Lull commented. "They're not usually so friendly."

"I'm sure they can tell that I love animals," I replied, rubbing between each horse's ears. "They're both beautiful."

Lull set about harnessing the horses to a hitch wagon. She carefully positioned the collar of the harnesses on each horse so that the weight of the wagon would be evenly distributed on their shoulders and chests. She clipped the lead rope to the halter, then placed the hames on top of the collar and tightened it.

I helped her center the saddles and breeching on each horse's back. Then Lull arranged the traces to point toward the horses' rears. She threaded the reins through the saddle guides and attached the cruppers beneath the horses' tails. After Lull had bridled the horses and attached the reins to the bits, I pulled the wagon to the rear of the horses.

Finally, Lull connected the traces to the wagon, and we were ready to go to market.

I thought about how easily we Humans simply get into our cars and go wherever we want without a thought. Just going to the market was a major project here in Faerie. Life was simpler – but also harder.

Lull and I settled ourselves on the wooden seat of the wagon. Lull clucked her tongue and signaled the horses with a flick of the reins. The horses moved forward in tandem, obviously experienced workers.

The spoke wheels bumped over the uneven ground as we took the dirt road into Agrarian Lea. The horses' hooves, squeaky wheels, and jarring of the wagon made conversation difficult, so I concentrated on the scenery.

It was a crisp autumn day, cool but not cold, the sun shining in an almost cloudless sky. We passed dormant fields interspersed with meadows where black and white cattle, shaggy goats, gold and white horses, and spotted deer grazed contentedly together.

I realized that I was seeing Earth as it would be if not for the Industrial Revolution. What would happen to Faerie if technology suddenly invaded this primitive, agricultural society? While physical life would be easier with the help of machinery, was the destruction of the environment worth the physical convenience? I hoped Faerie would never find out.

It was a beautiful scene, peaceful even, but suddenly I shivered. The back of my neck prickled as the short hairs at my nape stood up in alarm. I looked back, but there was no one behind the wagon. I felt watched by an unfriendly gaze, all the same.

As we approached the village, I saw that the wood and straw buildings I had seen from Lull's cottage were barns, sheds, and animal pens. The buildings in the village itself were breathtaking.

Residential and commercial structures were made of stone, some with bits of embedded quartz that reflected the light in thousands of tiny sparkles. As we drove past, I marveled at the etchings of leaves, flowers, trees, and pastoral scenes that decorated them.

The small shops were welded together into long buildings on two sides of the common square. Arched porticos at each shop's entrance bore the names of the establishments. We passed a baker, clothier, apothecary, pub, and candlemaker before my attention was stolen by the marketplace.

In the common area were dozens of tents and wooden stalls. The tents were composed of bright, colorful fabrics that competed with each other for notice. The aisles were busy with shoppers carrying cloth bags or baskets. I smiled. This could be any flea market back at home, except that some of these shoppers had wings, or extra arms, or pointed ears.

Lull parked the wagon and climbed down. She tied the horses to a rail alongside a few similar rigs. I joined her, still ogling the incredible architecture and exotic Fairies. Their clothing was eye-catching. The small female Fae wore flower petals sewn together into dresses and garlands of flowers or matching flower-petal caps on their heads. The males wore shirts and pants woven from sheep's wool.

Larger Fae wore clothing that looked like it belonged on baby dolls, or was made from cotton. Human-sized Fae were dressed according to their races – Elves wore green tunics and leggings, woodland creatures wore clothing in browns and reds, and others I couldn't identify looked completely Human in form and dress.

"Stay with me, Miss Odessa. It's easy to get lost in these crowds," Lull counseled as she handed me a shopping basket.

I followed Lull into the tumult that was the market. It was a cacophony of sounds and sights. Vendors barked, Fae yelled over each other, different sources of live music were competing. I didn't know where to look first.

Lull led me to a tent and I waited behind her. The tent flaps bore an extensive variety of hair clips in plastic, metal, and silk flowers.

Some were in pairs but the majority were singles. On a narrow table at the front of the tent were shallow baskets filled with bobby pins, ribbons, barrettes, clawtooth clips, ponytail holders, and one large basket of hairbands.

Lull chose a pair of barrettes encrusted with rhinestones and began bargaining with the vendor. He was small, wrinkled, and bald, with dark skin and eyes. His movements were very quick, as were his speech and darting eyes. He gazed soulfully at Lull as he explained that he could take no less for jewelry of such caliber.

I lost interest in the sale and watched the passing browsers. I was surprised to see that many Fae looked no different than the average Human. I had expected all Fae to be small, but my stereotype was very wrong. They were shorter than me, taller than me, fat, thin, long-haired or bald. Some were obviously family while others were packs of young people. Couples held hands as they walked. Young mothers carried infants in slings or led children through the throngs.

It looked so normal that I half-forgot where I was – until I would glimpse the edge of a wing, an uncommonly-colored eye, or elongated, pointed ears. A flock of Sprites hovering over the heads of those blocking their view into a tent were a quick reminder that this was Faerie, after all.

The shopping basket I was holding pulled out of my relaxed grip. It fell and landed on its side in the dirt at my feet. The Fae who had knocked it out of my grasp just stood there. He didn't seem to care about what he'd done. I reached for the basket. A heavy leather boot crunched down on the basket.

"I do apologize," a man's cheery voice said.

I looked up into the pallid face of a young man. He was thin but muscular, wearing a semi-transparent metallic shirt over leather pants and knee-high boots. He looked Human, with short brown hair brushed away from his high forehead. His eyes were dark and glittery and rings of dark, ashy skin circled them. His eyes were too close together and crowded his predominant nose. He smiled falsely, making the gesture a vague threat.

44

"It's all right," I replied despite my annoyance.

I grasped the basket handle as his pale hand closed over mine. His touch was hot, and I jerked away.

"It appears I have damaged it," he noted with a happy lilt to his voice.

"Yes, you did." I showed him the crushed side of the basket.

He was making me nervous. I didn't like how he stood there glaring at me, his words happily hostile. I met his eyes and a bone-chill slid down my torso, making me actually shiver. This was the same unfriendly gaze I had sensed during the ride into town.

Despite having no idea what I was going to say, I opened my mouth to speak, but before I could he turned on his bootheel, stepped into the throng of passersby, and was gone. I gaped after him, clutching the broken basket.

"Look!" Lull shook my arm. "Look, I got them!" She held out the barrettes, then looked at me. "What's wrong, Miss Odessa?"

"That ugly man stomped my basket on purpose." For some reason I couldn't define, I wanted to burst into tears.

"He did? Well, don't pay any mind to that. We can get you another one." Lull said, patting my shoulder.

I took the barrettes from Lull and clipped them to the ends of her braids. She laughed and preened, and I found myself laughing, too. I was becoming fond of my companion. She was the only person in this alien land that I was comfortable with. I would tell Lull the details of the incident after we returned home, rather than let it continue to spoil my day.

Home, I thought wonderingly, *I've been here less than a day and I'm already saying home.*

There wasn't much time to dwell on the altercation as we resumed our marketing. Lull purchased a new basket from a lovely Fae who was demonstrating basketweaving in front of her stall. It seemed only natural that she should practice this art as she was tall, slender, and willowy. Her light brown hair flowed to her knees and her wings were pale blue. Creamy skin set off her azure eyes. Her twin brother, the only difference being his dark blue wings, handled sales as she entranced watchers with her deft, sure fingers weaving willow branches into complex patterns.

Lull handed me the willow basket she had just purchased. "Keep it. It's yours."

I smiled and thanked her, aware that to refuse the gift would be insulting.

We moved on to the next tent, situated at the end of the row. Beside it, three male Fae played a violin, a drum, and a strange stringed instrument I had never seen before. They accompanied two barefoot female dancers. This group reminded me of gypsies. The musicians wore dark pants and full-sleeved shirts under red vests. They laughed and shouted as they played, turning their joy into music. The turbaned dancers wore flowing, multi-layered skirts in bright colors that swirled around their lithe bodies.

"What is that?" I pointed to the Fae seated on the ground tapping the strings of an instrument with four legs. He held a wooden hammer in each hand. Each hammer head was wrapped with leather.

"That's a cimbalom," Lull said briskly, taking my arm. She leaned in close. "Hold onto anything you value around the Ronickels. They'll rob you between blinks."

Lull dragged me away as I looked over my shoulder at the laughing, dancing troupe. We rounded the corner and my gaze was drawn to the next seller.

He was very tall, well over six feet. His skin glowed with a gold hue. He was bald and had pointed ears, from which grew the only hair on his body. He was nude but covered with tattoos from head to toe. Brightly colored geometric designs, creeping vines, landscapes, faces, animals, and neon blue polka dots the size of half-dollars all fought for attention.

I was busy deciphering the designs for a few moments before I noticed the clutch of knives in his large hand. He slung one of the knives at a similar Fae standing in front of a wooden backdrop. The blade of the knife embedded itself into the wood barely an inch from the Fae's left eye. He didn't even blink.

"This is the Dirk, the Knife Tribe." Lull explained. "I get all of my knives from them. You can't find a better kitchen knife. You can slice a potato just by dropping it on the blade."

I studied the knives. They were works of art. Constructed from one piece of metal, they were 12 inches long with decorative etchings on the handles. The blades were wide at the base but narrowed to a sharp point. Both edges of the blade had been sharpened.

With amazing speed and precision, the Dirk hurled all of the throwing knives at his target. They met the woodboard with solid "thunks," all of them spaced evenly around the target Dirk's head. I clapped, then realized I was the only one applauding and stopped, embarrassed. A few Fae looked at me curiously but then moved on.

"I keep forgetting I'm not at home anymore," I confided to Lull.

"That's to the good," Lull replied. "There's no reason this couldn't become your home, is there?"

I turned sharply. "What do you mean?"

Lull reddened. "I'm sorry, Miss Odessa. I only meant that – that – oh, lamb's buttocks, I don't know what I meant."

I smiled and gave the woman a quick hug. "It's all right. I know you mean no harm. And actually, you're right. There's not a lot back at home to keep me there … but that doesn't mean I want to stay here."

Lull smiled and led me down the aisle to our next stop. I peeked around browsing Fae into every tent we passed. The array of items for sale was as amusing as it was eclectic.

One stall sold socks, all sizes, colors, and materials, but only one of each. Another sold "collectible coins" that I saw were Human currency – pennies, nickels, dimes, and quarters. One displayed an assortment of writing pens which, for the smaller Fae, could serve as weapons, I realized, as I watched two Pixies playfully duel with them. At another stall, a group of female Fae were sorting through a basket of scarves, holding them up against each other's faces to test the colors.

Hair clips. Socks. Pens. Loose change. Scarves. I laughed aloud. A mystery had just been solved. This was where all the items that Humans "lost" ended up. The old saying that Pixies had stolen whatever item was missing was actually true. At last, the puzzle of how only one sock got lost "in the dryer" had been solved.

Chapter 5
Traveling Shovel of Death

I saw some fabric that would look just beautiful on you, Miss Odessa. Would you care to see it?" Lull inquired with a hopeful look on her face.

"I don't know how to sew," I replied.

Lull laughed. "I'll make you a dress. I love to sew. It'll be delightful to have someone else besides myself to sew for. Allow me this little good turn, won't you?"

"All right," I answered.

Lull's face brightened. "Come, then," she urged. "We must hurry before someone else gets your fabric."

As I followed Lull down the aisle, singing caught my attention. I saw a young man playing a lute as he sang a mournful tune. His black tunic was striped with fuzzy red piping. His pants were a soft red, and a square red cap sat atop his shaggy black hair. I stopped to listen, ignoring Lull's impatient tug on my arm. Something about the boy, or the song, or both, demanded my witness … and not mine alone. A crowd was gathering at the front of the tent, pushing Lull and me closer to the boy as he crooned in a sweet, soul-stirring voice.

"Morning and evening Fairies heard the Humans cry:
'Come buy our orchard fruits, Come buy, come buy:
Apples and quinces, plump unpecked cherries,
Melons and raspberries, swart-headed mulberries,
Wild free-born cranberries,crabapples, dewberries,

Blackberries, strawberries —
all ripe together in summer weather.'
Evening by evening among the brookside rushes,
Fey bowed their heads to hear,
Crouching close together in the cooling weather,
With clasping arms and cautioning lips,
with tingling cheeks and fingertips,
'Lie close,' Fey Mother said, pricking up her golden head:
'We must not look at Human men,
We must not buy their fruits;
Who knows upon what soil they fed.'

But sweet-tooth Fey child spoke in haste:
'Human folk, I have no coin; I have no copper in my purse,
I have no silver either.'
'You have much gold upon your head,' they answered together:
'Buy from us with a golden curl.'
She clipped a precious golden lock,
She dropped a tear more rare than pearl,
Then sucked their fruit globes fair or red:

Clearer than water flowed that juice;
she never tasted such before,
She sucked until her lips were sore;
then flung the emptied rinds away,
She turned home alone and knew not was it night or day.
Day after day, night after night, Fey Child kept watch in vain,
In sullen silence of exceeding pain.
She never caught again the Human cry: 'Come buy, come buy.'

But ever in the moonlight she pined and pined away;
Sought them by night and day,
Found them no more, but dwindled and grew gray;
Then fell with the first snow,
While to this day no grass will grow where she lies low."

The boy finished, the lute stopped, and the only sounds were of sobbing. Tears streamed down faces both coarse and beautiful. No one within sound of the song was spared.

A woman strode up to the boy from the back of the tent, obviously angry.

"How many times have I told you not to do that?" she demanded as she jerked the lute out of his hands.

"Awww, Mother. It's just so boring watching the tent!" he complained, reaching for the instrument.

She held it away from him. "You release them. Right now. Every one of them! Or you'll never see this thing again!"

The boy sighed. He faced us and made a gesture. Around me, Fae began regaining their composure. Some wiped their faces curiously, unaware of why they had been crying. I was surprised to see that the small group had become much larger. The music's magic had spellbound anyone who passed by and heard it and had lured them to join the group. The small group had become a crowd.

The mother grabbed the unrepentant boy and marched him into the back of the tent, cuffing him as they walked.

Lull mopped her face with her apron. "I should have known," she grumped. "A Siren. I hate it when this happens. Crying gives me a headache."

"I can't stop crying," I said, rubbing my eyes.

"You're Human. It'll probably take you a little longer," Lull reassured me.

As I wiped my eyes, I noticed that many of the throng that stood near us were now pointing at me and whispering to each other. Embarrassed, I averted my gaze.

A Flower Fairy and her child approached and I moved aside to allow them to pass. Grateful to have something other than the gossipers to focus on, I admired the Fairies as they came close. The mother wore poppy leaves wound around her torso, their jagged edges smoothed down. Her skirt and her hair were poppy-red and her wings shone poppy-yellow in the bright sunlight. Dark eyes the color of poppy stamen flashed in my direction and then away. She led the child by the hand and quickened her steps as they grew nearer.

The child was a miniature of her mother with the exception that her clothing was all made of leaves. The child looked up at me and her eyes widened. She stopped abruptly, causing her mother to lurch to a stop.

"Mama, look! A round-ears!"

The mother glared at me as though I had done something to her child.

"Come away," she snapped, and scooped up the child in her arms. She hurried past us and was swallowed by the crowd.

Watching them, I realized that the crowd had drawn closer around us.

"Round-ears," someone jeered.

"Round-ears," someone else snarled.

Those pressing close to us began to chant and hoot.

"Round-ears. Round-ears. Round-ears..."

"Lull, let's go now," I said, shamed and hurt.

I looked for a path out of the suddenly threatening crowd of Fae.

"Stop it!" Lull screamed, causing me to start with fright. "Stop it right now!"

The chanting lessened slightly but didn't immediately stop.

"You should all be ashamed of yourselves!" Lull yelled, her plump face now a dull red and tears of anger brightening her eyes. "How dare you treat a guest of Gildan like this?"

The chanting stopped and those Fae nearest us suddenly looked uneasy.

"Begone, all of you. You have shamed no one but yourselves."

Lull grabbed my hand and pulled me alongside of her as she walked out of the crowd, defiantly meeting the eyes of all who watched as we stepped onto the main pathway of the market.

"What was that all about? I thought Humans and Fairies got along – why do they dislike me so much?"

"I'm so sorry that happened, Odessa," Lull sighed. "This is exactly why Gildan placed you with me. Some Folk are less evolved than others. Humans and Fairies were enemies in the far past. Some Folks have long memories and short manners."

She shook her head sadly. "They tried to shame you but only succeeded in shaming themselves. There will be even more shame to bear once Gildan hears of this."

"Oh, there's no need to bother Gildan," I protested. My body was still shaking off the adrenalin surge but I wasn't ready to make the incident more than it was.

Lull smiled and ignored my protest. "Let's get our minds off such ugly business. Let's go find the perfect fabric for your dress, shall we?"

I allowed Lull to change the subject and followed her down the path but my mind was still uneasy and working on a vague problem. Something still wasn't right but I couldn't place what it was.

Then, as music from a nearby entertainment began, I realized what was bothering me. The song – the Siren's song – if Humans and the Fey were no longer at odds, why had the song featured Humans as the enemy? I started to ask Lull but she had spotted the tailor's tent and was hustling toward it too quickly for me to question her.

"Black?" I fingered the material Lull presented to me for inspection. "I'm not sure I want a black dress."

Lull held part of the fabric up into the light. "See how it shimmers? It'll positively glow in the moonlight," she argued. "And look at the detail."

I had to admit that the black-on-black embroidery was stunning. Silver threads peeped from the embellishment, twinkling like stars in a midnight sky.

"It will be just the thing for WintersFeast," Lull said excitedly.

"A winter party?"

"Oh, yes. It's the most exciting time of the year," Lull explained. "All of Faery feasts and celebrates The Goddess of the Hunt. At the end of the feast there's a symbolic hunt."

"What gets hunted?"

"Oh, that's done by lottery." Lull's face darkened for just a moment. "WintersFeast is a grand tradition. You'll have a fine time – if you're still here."

I couldn't bring myself to dampen Lull's enthusiasm, despite my not being really pleased with the dress material.

"All right. I'm sure this will make a lovely dress, and if I'm still here, I'll be honored to wear it."

With a delighted giggle, Lull scooped up the bolt of fabric and zoned in on the vendor. As I looked at the other materials for sale, the jam of shoppers temporarily thinned and I caught sight of two Pixies making mischief in the opposite tent.

The vendor, a young woman, had fallen asleep in her chair. The Pixies were busily tying knots in her long red hair, giggling and goading each other into more and more complicated knots.

I walked over to them. They were so preoccupied with their game that they didn't notice me until I spoke.

"Shame on you," I scolded. "You're ruining her beautiful hair."

The Pixies startled as one and looked up at me with big, guilty eyes. The prank, while annoying, was essentially harmless. I leaned over them and gently shook the woman from her impromptu nap.

"It's best not to close your eyes with Pixies around," I said. "These two have been playing with your hair."

The young woman blinked, then saw the tangles. She jumped to her feet.

"You hedge-born, pribbling worm-sons!" she cried.

Now more frightened of her than they were of me, the Pixies hid behind my legs. They peeped at the woman as she flailed angrily at her hair.

"Stop, stop, you're making it worse," I said, catching her hands. "Sit down. Let me help you." The woman calmed as I began picking out the knots closest to me.

"I'm Vermilion," the woman said as she carefully untied a tangle. "I know better than to fall asleep here."

She glared at the Pixies still peeking around me. "Did you Dust me, too?"

"Oh, no," one of the Pixies insisted. "You were already asleep. That's why we got the idea."

"That's a likely story," Vermilion replied, but her voice was much less angry.

"I could use some help here," I said to the Pixies. "You two did a very good job."

The second Pixie shook his head with vehemence. "If we get too close, she will squash us!"

"No she won't," I assured them, then turned to Vermilion. "Will you?"

Vermilion rolled her eyes. "It will be hard, but I will try to control myself."

I stepped back and gestured at the Pixies. "Well? Get busy."

The Pixies looked at each other, then at Vermilion. She ignored them, busy with her hair. They flew up onto the table and began undoing their work.

They had almost finished the job when Lull entered the tent.

"Pillyswiggin and Gollysnuffle, what have you done this time?"

Gollysnuffle pointed at Pillyswiggin. "He made me do it!"

"Did not! It was your idea!"

The Pixies continued to squabble and shove each other as they followed Lull and me out of the tent.

"I can't wait to get started on your dress," Lull commented as we began to walk. "I have just one more stop before we go home."

Lull led me to a stall selling buttons and immersed herself in a search for the perfect match to the newly purchased fabric. After a moment or two, I wandered to a nearby tent to examine a collection of metal tools, cups, weapons, and eating utensils.

Behind the display tables were two Dwarves. They were built like small mountains. One wore chain mail and heavy boots; the other simple brown pants and shirt with soft boots. Both had long pigtails and beards, one white and one brown.

"Everything here is handmade," grunted the brown-haired Dwarf in the simple clothing.

"I can see that. It's all beautiful," I said, admiring a finely-etched drinking cup.

I came to the garden tools and reached for a shovel, wondering if Lull might be interested in it for use in her garden.

"Don't touch that!" yelled the white-haired Dwarf. "No touching or else ya buy it!"

"Well, excuse me," I replied, offended.

"Don't chase the customers away, Brutus," chided the brown-haired Dwarf, slapping his companion heartily on the back as he passed. "I'm sorry, Miss. That really is something you don't want to touch. It's the Dwarfish TSOD, ya see."

"TSOD?"

"The Traveling Shovel of Death. See there?" He pointed to the shovel's blade.

There was a stain of brownish-red substance that was darker than rust.

"That's blood. It's permanent. Won't come off no matter what."

"Oh." I stepped back, unsure whether I was being told the truth or being conned. "What would happen if I touched it?"

Brutus hawked and spit. "What always happens. You'd hack off a head or a leg or something – probably one of ours, but it don't matter none whose. Then it would go after you until you got rid of it. That's how it travels."

I smiled at the tall tale. "So which one of you killed someone with it?"

56

Brutus winked, said nothing.

I left, still unsure whether or not my leg was being pulled.

It had been hours since we had arrived at the market, and I was getting tired and hungry. I saw an unoccupied bench tucked under a tree and sat down to rest my tired feet.

I set the basket down beside the bench and watched for Lull to emerge from the button tent. I watched the crowds of Fae pass me by. A quick glimpse of black caught my eye and I saw a cat darting through the sea of legs. It was a Tuxedo cat that looked just like …

"Milk Monster?" I said the name questioningly and the cat's ears pricked. She weaved her way out of the crowd and trotted over to me, tail held high. "Monster! It can't be you! How in the world did you get here?"

She purred and rubbed my legs as I ran my hand down her back. "I can't believe this. It really is you!"

My mind raced. If Milk Monster could get here, she could get OUT. Unless – unless she had come along with me somehow and was now also trapped. How could I find out?

I leaned to lift Milk Monster onto my lap but she squirmed away and darted under the bench. I stood up and looked under the bench but she was gone. *Dammit! I need to know if she knows the way home!*

My mind returned to my predicament. When would Gildan meet with the Silver Company? How long would it take for them to make a decision? Would they allow me to go home? And what would I do if they declined? I had no idea how I was brought here, much less how to find my way out of Faery on my own. *Maybe I could throw myself on the mercy of the Company*, I thought gloomily. *Do the Fae even know what mercy is?*

Would it be so horrible to stay here? It's so beautiful and the Fae have been friendly – well, mostly friendly – so far. Maybe I could sell my pottery here at the market. I could pit-fire it, or even build a stone kiln. Surely there would be fuel here that would reach 1950 degrees. Maybe even a magic spell …

My thoughts were interrupted as a blond man carrying a Pixie by the collar approached me.

"Miss, I believe this belongs to you," the panting blond man said.

I thought he meant the Pixie and started to object but then saw that the Pixie was holding a jar of fig jam. I looked down into my basket to confirm and saw that Lull's jar of fig jam was gone.

"I saw him take it out of your basket and chased him. He's a fast little puttock!"

The Pixie squirmed.

"You are not going anywhere until you give the lady back what you stole from her," the man said, emphasizing his words with a shake.

"All right, all right!" the Pixie yelled, his little face turning purple. "Here!"

He thrust the jar toward me. I took it from him and returned it to the basket. Nothing else appeared to be missing.

"Let me go!" the Pixie shrieked, "I gave it back!"

The blond man looked to me and I nodded. He released the Pixie who flew away, filling the air behind him with curses.

"Thank you for saving Lull's jam," I said with a grateful smile.

The man gestured toward the bench. "Do you mind? I am a bit winded. I am not used to chasing Pixies."

"Please." I indicated that he should sit down. "I'm Odessa."

"Pretty name," the man said as he leaned back on the bench. "I am Adram. I have not seen you here before, and I come to market every week."

"I'm – I'm visiting," I said, glancing toward the button tent. Still no Lull; however, I saw the thieving Pixie pushing his brother inside. No doubt the vendor would soon be missing part of his inventory.

"So what do you do when you are not being robbed by Pixies?"

I hesitated. "I work with clay. And you?"

The young man stretched languidly before answering, as if giving me time to admire him. His waist-length hair was gathered into a low ponytail and held by a leather thong. His features were strong and surprisingly human – no slanted eyes or pointed ears. His busy turquoise eyes, however, belied his casual pose. He wore a forest green tunic over brown suede pants and short leather boots.

"I am an officer of politics, and I am sure you have no interest in discussing the political issues of a place you are but visiting," he replied, winking at me.

"I can't imagine there are serious issues in a place as idyllic as Faerie," I answered.

"And the lady confirms that she is, indeed, a tourist," Adram laughed – then grew serious. "Look around you. How many species have you seen? This is but a small sample of the exotica that is Faerie. You cannot have this much diversity without some conflict."

"I suppose that's true. Conflict is a daily occurrence back at home, and our number of races is much smaller."

Adram turned toward me. "Let us not dwell on conflict. I do enough of that as it is." He smiled charmingly. "Will you be here for WintersFeast?"

I looked away. "I really don't know."

"Oh, if you can, you must come! It's one of Faerie's finest moments … and the best food you will ever eat."

"So I've heard."

"There is a huge feast with every kind of meat, cheese, vegetable, and dessert you can imagine. Folks bring it from all over the lands. There are entertainments, games, singers, music, and of course, dancing. Lots and lots of dancing. And did I mention the food?"

We both laughed.

"It does sound wonderful," I admitted.

"It is," he assured me. "It would be a wonderful way for someone who is visiting to see a little bit of all Faerie has to offer. It would most certainly be worth your time to stay for it, I promise you."

He paused as though thinking, then slid across the bench beside me. "Would you consider accompanying me to WintersFeast?" His turquoise eyes held mine for a moment, then dropped, suddenly shy.

I smiled. This handsome young man was actually flirting with me – but why? I couldn't imagine that of all of the gorgeous Fae women I'd seen today that he preferred an overweight, graying, older woman. Could he sense that I was Human and wanted to indulge his curiosity? After all, he had to have been born long after the last Human lived in Faerie.

"Thank you for the invitation, Adram, but I'll most likely be back at home by the time WintersFeast comes."

His downcast eyes snapped back up to mine. Now there was anger flaring in them. The turquoise melted away and was replaced by a dark, smoky brown. His facial features transformed into a sickeningly familiar pale face with crowded features and brown hair. The man who had deliberately destroyed my basket for no reason was now seated next to me. At this moment, however, there was no more fake cheer to his ugly disposition.

I gasped and jumped to my feet.

"You!" I cried. "What do you want?"

The Pixies pulled Lull out of the button tent by her skirt. She was fighting them, fussing and slapping at their grasping hands, until she caught sight of Adram and me.

Adram smiled nastily as he stood up slowly and faced me. His malevolent eyes darted at Lull and the Pixies, who were all now running toward us. Lull was trying to run and rummage in her shopping basket at the same time.

Adram snarled and pointed a clawed fingernail at me. "What I want is you, Human! I shall have you, make no mistake about that."

"Begone, Changeling!" Lull shrieked as she flung a handful of white crystals on the menacing figure. Adram spasmed, brushing furiously at his clothing. With one murderous glance at Lull, he vanished.

"That's right, run, you malt-worm!" Pillyswiggin peed Fairie Dust into the space where Adram had last stood.

"And don't come back!" Gollysnuffle yelled, joining his brother in the Dust-fest.

"Are you all right?" Lull cried, dropping her basket and grabbing me by the arms. "Did he hurt you?"

Her frantic eyes searched my body.

"I'm – I'm all right," I assured her with a shaking voice.

Lull hugged me. "Thank the Gods I just bought some salt."

Lull and I collapsed on the bench. Lull clutched her chest. My whole body shook.

"Who was that?" I demanded.

Lull started to speak, then looked at the Pixies, who were competing with each other's curse words.

"Pixies, shoo!" she said. "Stop that, or I'll salt you, too."

Pillyswiggin and Gollysnuffle laughed at the empty threat. Salt was harmless to them.

Lull got up and stomped threateningly. Gollysnuffle stopped in mid-curse and ran underneath the bench. Pillyswiggin followed when he realized Lull was serious.

"Shoo, or I'll take a switch to you," Lull said as she bent to look under the bench.

Satisfied that they were indeed gone, she reseated herself.

"That, Miss Odessa, was a Changeling." She shook her head. "They don't come around very often. I can't imagine what brought this one up from the Darklands."

"He said he was a politician of sorts. Then he said he was here for me. Why would he want me? He didn't make it sound like a good thing. I haven't done anything to him – or anyone else in Faerie, for that matter."

Lull looked at me with a thoughtful expression. "Perhaps it's because you're a Human. Perhaps Gildan has already met with the Company and that's how the Changelings became aware of you."

"There's a Changeling in the Company?"

Lull nodded. "Every benevolent or neutral species is represented in the Silver Company. Changelings aren't evil enough to be banned, but also are not benevolent enough to be totally trusted."

"As for Adram, he has a sad history. He was switched with a Human baby, as is Changeling custom, but his Human parents rejected him. They sent him to what you Humans call an orphanage. He never spoke of his experiences there but it seems to have fed his anger and resentment toward Humans."

"After orphanage, he joined a group of Human criminals and his behavior escalated into violence. He ended up being sentenced to a Human prison for life, but as you know, no Human prison can hold a Changeling. It was decided to bring him back to Faerie so that he wouldn't be found out."

"Wasn't he grateful to come back here?"

"No, he blames the Folk for trading him to begin with. I think the anger runs too deep in him to ever change. He has been nurturing that anger for at least a century."

"Well, at least now I know he would have acted badly toward any Human, not just me. That makes me feel a little better."

"We shall have to consult Gildan when we get home. He'll see to it that the Changeling leaves you alone."

"Oh, no, don't worry Gildan with this," I protested.

"He would want to know." Lull reached out and gave me a quick hug. "Don't you worry. You're safe with me. He won't come back. I have a whole package of salt."

I sighed. "This has been a strange day." That remark reminded me of Monster. "Lull, do cats come here from my world?"

She nodded. "Sometimes. Cats are of both worlds, don't you know? They come and go as they please, as far as I can tell. Shall we go home now? Are you hungry? I am." She picked up her shopping bag and basket.

"Lunch sounds wonderful." Not really knowing why, I was reluctant to tell Lull that I had seen Milk Monster. It was something I felt was best kept to myself for now.

I retrieved my basket from under the bench and couldn't believe my eyes. The jar of fig jam was gone – again.

Chapter 6
The Silver Company

Gildan the Silver approached the door to the Company chambers. It was an arched wood door, the arch coming to a point at the top. The door was set into a wall of stone barely taller than the door itself. Foliage draped from cracks and pockets in the wall, created by time and weather.

Gildan opened the door and stepped into an outdoor courtyard studded with large trees. Amongst the trees were rows of wooden benches that almost filled the courtyard. This was where the Fae representatives witnessed or participated in the Silver Company meetings.

There were already some in attendance. Gildan passed a group of Elves, one of whom caught his eye and nodded. Dryads could be seen as outlines in their trees. Dream-Devourers and Butterfly Faeries flew overhead as Goblins and Fire Fae and Gnomes chattered among themselves. Gildan noted a Brain-Gobbler sitting alone and staring at the backs of others' heads.

Pixies chased and tumbled in the aisles between the benches. Firefly Fae pulsed and Sky-Dancers perched on small branches of the centuries-old oaks, joining Skodsra in their preferred form as owls.

On the right side of the benches was a saltwater pond for the comfort of the water Fae. Dragonfly Fae darted above the heads of Mermaids and Nix. Water Sprites dangled their legs into the water as they sat on the edges of lily pads.

Facing the benches was a rectangular table and four wooden chairs. The first of the leaders to arrive, Gildan took his assigned seat, facing the benches, as indicated by a silver place card. He arranged his green and silver robe and waited for the three remaining Lords and Ladies of the Silver Company to arrive.

He had barely made himself comfortable when the door to the courtyard opened, revealing Poseida, the leader of the Undines, the Water-Fae.

She moved like poured liquid to the table. Her ocean-blue robe and headdress of veils whispered like surf with her movements. The silk fabric, embossed with water crystals, set off her creamy skin and large, green, up-slanted eyes.

"Poseida, you are as lovely as ever," Gildan greeted her.

She smiled and approached the seat to his left. "Lord Gildan. We have an unusual matter before us today."

"Yes, yes, we do," he chuckled.

Again the courtyard door opened and this time Tempestra, leader of the Sylphs, crossed the threshold. She appeared to float, her buttery yellow robe drifting in invisible currents around her. Large, silver, sparkling wings framed her tall and slender body. Blonde hair fell to her waist. Expressive blue eyes twinkled as she greeted Gildan and Poseida with her usual cheerful smile.

"I am most eager to learn more about this Human in our midst," she said with a airy wave. "I never expected this would happen again. I thought our dealings with Humans were long over."

She sat beside Poseida and took a sip from a glass of carbonated water. "Oh Gildan, the next time you go to BacchusYard, you must bring back some of this for me. I love how it tickles my nose." She giggled.

Tempestra couldn't sit still and was easily distracted, yet she managed to follow the proceedings most of the time. Her decisions were impulsive and easily changed, so Gildan felt she would be easily persuaded to take his side in allowing Odessa to live and return to Earth.

Poseida, however, was Tempestra's opposite. Poseida was a still pool, observing everything around her. She was serious and thoughtful, and her temper, when roused, was frightening. It would take some work to win her.

The assemblage had become restless by the time Adram, the leader of the Fire Fae, strode into the gathering. His unbuttoned red robe billowed behind him like flames. The skin around his eyes was black, as though the fire in his dark eyes had burnt rings of ash around them. The remainder of his face was pale against the darkness. He sat with a flourish, not acknowledging his fellow officers.

"Let us get this thing under way," he said, as though he had been the one waiting for a latecomer.

Gildan ignored the comment and stood. "I now call the meeting to order."

The courtyard quieted almost immediately. A couple of Goblins continued to grumble until a Dryad in the nearest tree smacked one of them with a branch.

"As you all probably know, there is a Human in Faerie. The last time we hosted a Human was 300 years ago."

"And fine slaves they were, too!" called one of the Elves. "It's a shame they wear out so quickly!"

There was laughter that quickly withered under Gildan's glare.

"I will have order. This is an important matter that deserves the respect of all in attendance."

Adram rolled his eyes. "Only to you," he muttered into his sleeve.

"The Human, Odessa Chase, is living on my homestead under the guardianship of Lull. The purpose of today's meeting is to decide whether to return her to the Earthly Realm or use her as prey in The Wild Hunt."

"Why is there a question?" Poseida asked. "If she can be of use in The Wild Hunt, why should we return her to Earth?"

"The problem is, Lady Poseida, that she has Sight."

There was a collective gasp from the spectators.

"I do not believe we should waste her talent in The Wild Hunt, but instead use it for our own good," Gildan continued. "This first came to my attention when the Pixie Pillyswiggin reported that she saw him in the Earthly Realm. I did not believe him at first. Then I went to her home and witnessed myself that she does have Sight. Since the plight of Faerie is ever on my mind, it occurred to me that she could be useful to us, so I had the Pixies Dust her and I brought her here."

"But how can that be?" Tempestra questioned, rescuing her carbonated water from some curious Sky Dancers. "There hasn't been a Human with Sight for a thousand years. What makes this one special?"

"I do not know," Gildan admitted. "However she got it, it is her talent. In the past, Humans who returned home and spoke of us were deemed mad. There were no consequences to allowing them to return. However, this case is different."

"I cannot stress enough to you how much the Earth and Humans have changed since those days. There is a chance that should she return home and speak of us with fear, that other Humans will follow her back here, led by her Sight. Humans have their own magics now, magics that could destroy us, I am sure."

The assemblage began rumbling like low thunder.

"Listen to me. I propose that we make a friend of this Human. Show her the damage that Humans are doing to Faerie since they lost their Sight. We can't hide it behind Glamour forever. You know that. She can take our message of distress to the Earthly Realm and make them realize that the destruction of Earth is being copied here in Faerie. I have been doing a lot of thinking about this, and I believe Odessa Chase is the answer from the Gods."

"One puny Human?" Adram snorted. "You are delusional, Gildan. Humans are nothing but slaves and breeders. Yet this one is living on your land. All I see is Gildan the Silver coddling a Human that we need for the Hunt."

Gildan's posture stiffened and his silver eyes gleamed with smoldering anger. "Lord Adram, you will have your opportunity to speak. I wish to present my case without interruption."

Adram gestured toward him with an upright palm. "By all means."

Gildan faced the assembly once more. "We all know that Faerie is in trouble. Our environment is deteriorating alongside that of its sister Earth. Our air is not as sweet. Our livestock – and even we – are suffering ill health. The trees and crops are sickened. We can keep covering this up with Glamour, but eventually even that will not be enough to cover the suffering."

"I agree, Lord Gildan," Poseida spoke up. "Our waters are starting to show signs of sickness and an inability to support the forms of life that are vital to us."

"Yes, yes," called a Mermaid. "It is becoming harder to find fish and frogs for food."

The Sprites nodded vigorously in agreement with her.

"The flowers are not as lush as they were," Tempestra piped up. "The pollen and nectar are not as sweet and rich. The creatures of the air go hungry at times."

A Butterfly Fairie landed on her arm as she spoke, as if in confirmation. "You have no idea how hard it is to fly when you have low energy!" she continued. "I just hate that. I have to find twice as much to eat and I am still weak. And what if eating so much makes me fat? How will I fly then?"

Gildan held up a quieting hand. "I know this is so. I believe the remedy is to lower the Glamour so that the Human can see what Faerie really looks like. Then, when we return her to the Earthly Realm, she can tell the other Humans. Surely they will help us and themselves by limiting the destruction of both natural worlds."

Adram couldn't hold himself back. "You call this a remedy?" he cried. "How can one Human convince the multitudes who do not have the Sight?"

"Because, Lord Adram, the Earth has changed over time. Humans have created magic over communication. They no longer must be physically in the presence of another to speak with them. Odessa Chase can use this magic to tell the Earth of our plight," Gildan explained. "I have been there and have seen them do this."

"And I say so what?" Adram demanded. "So she tells them. Do you really believe the Humans will stop destroying their world on her say-so? Just to help us save ours? They are knowingly and deliberately ruining the place where they live, and you expect them to care about us?"

Adram laughed. "No wonder you are called Gildan the Silver. You believe everyone to be as pure as you!"

Tempestra held up a small hand. "Lord Adram, there is no need for personal attack," she chirped as the Butterfly Faerie fanned its wings for balance from its position on her finger. "Could I have another water, please? I do so love this water from BacchusYard. It is especially bubbly."

She giggled.

Gildan ignored her and pinned Adram with glowing eyes. "Since you have so little regard for my ideas, Lord Adram, perhaps you can regale us with your better solution?"

Adram leapt to his feet. "Actually I can. WintersFeast comes in but three months. Everyone here knows that the Huntress has no fealty for Faerie. She and her Huntsmen are not Folk. They have so little regard for our village that they destroy whatever is in their path just for the sake of destruction."

"Their history began with hunting Humans. This is our chance to offer them something they've been missing for a long, long time. Perhaps by giving them a Human to hunt they will spare our village for once. I say it is worth a try."

Chaos erupted among the assemblage. There were war-cries, cheers, hoots and screams of delight amid a cacophony of voices. Gildan was dismayed to see the majority so enthusiastic about the idea.

As soon as he had shouted down the noise and restored order, Adram again addressed them.

"This is an opportunity we cannot pass up. Why should we offer another Folk to the Huntress when we have a Human? Each Folk life is priceless. Humans can reproduce at will; they are expendable. If we save but one Folk, it will be worth it."

Again the spectators broke into cheers. Instead of calling order, Gildan allowed the noise to fade naturally. Then he turned to the Ladies.

"What say you to this?" he asked, feeling faint hope that the Ladies would be less bloodthirsty than the riled Fae in attendance.

Poseida stood first. "I agree with Lord Adram. I do not see how this one Human can persuade an entire world to change its ways. I am not convinced that even if they could see us, that they would care about our problems. They are relentlessly and eternally a very destructive race."

She paused, and tears formed in her sea-green eyes. "Perhaps the end of Faerie has been the plan of the Gods all along. Perhaps we were removed from the Earthly Realm for this very reason. Whatever reason the Gods have for favoring the Humans, we cannot change divine will."

"But is Faerie not worth the risk?" Gildan demanded. "Do we lie down and die without a fight? Do we keep painting a pretty picture on top of the decay and then simply cease to exist?"

"What choice do we have?" Adram countered. "Pinning the hopes of Faerie on one Human against the Gods is ridiculous! Only the Gods can turn back the damage that has been done, not the Humans. Our magic has been dying alongside our environment ever since the Humans inherited the Earthly Realm. We cannot win a battle with the Gods. I say if we must die, we die as hunters, not farmers!"

The crowd of Fae roared.

Tempestra stood up. "Oh, I have an idea. I was going to vote for the Hunt, but I have changed my mind. Lord Gildan, I propose that I meet with your Human and see for myself whether or not she is capable of such a task. I can deliver my findings and a final decision can then be made. Does that meet with your approval?"

She looked at him with wide expectant eyes.

Gildan knew he did not have the support of the Fae, but if Tempestra's WatchTower could be convinced, they could order Odessa's safety until she could return home with Faerie's message. He nodded.

"We will meet again in a few days."

Gildan stepped away from the table and left the courtyard. The Fae were still chattering excitedly. The words "Wild Hunt" echoed repeatedly behind him and his heavy heart battled hope in his chest.

Chapter 7
Faerie Glamour

Gildan knocked on the door of the cottage and then let himself in. Lull and I looked up from the table where we sat working on a list of recipes to prepare for WintersFeast.

"Lull, would you excuse Miss Odessa?"

He offered an arm to me. "Please take a walk with me."

Lull nodded. "Run along, dear. I can finish this."

I stood and took Gildan's proffered arm. We walked out of the cottage and onto the path that led to ToadSpit Lake. As we strolled in silence, I wondered when Gildan would tell me why he wanted to see me away from Lull. Unable to wait, I spoke first.

"When I was young, I used to dream about coming to Faerie," I said shyly. "Of course, I had no idea what it was really like."

He smiled. "You still do not," he replied gently. "There is much more to Faerie than what you see on the surface. Some of it good, some of it not."

"But you – you are good. I can tell."

Gildan laughed. "I am neither good nor bad. I am simply who and what I am. We do not see things in those terms like Humans do."

"What about evil, though? Do you recognize evil?" I asked, remembering the Changeling.

I had managed to put the incident at the market out of my mind for a while, but now it was back. I shuddered with the force of my feelings.

Gildan felt the tremors and stopped walking. "Why are you afraid?"

"Are Changelings evil? Lull says not, but I'm not so sure."

"When did you see a Changeling?" Gildan asked sharply, not answering my question.

I rushed through the story, eager to be rid of it.

"How did he threaten you?"

Gildan's body had gone stiff and his eyes were glowing as if on fire.

"I don't remember exactly. Something about 'I will have you,' I think. It doesn't make any sense! I'd never seen him before, much less done anything to make him want to hurt me."

Gildan forcibly relaxed his tense posture and patted my hand.

"You need not fear him. I will take care of this," he said in a reassuring tone. "Changelings are ..." he searched for the right word, "... impudent. I will see to it that he does not bother you again."

I smiled at him. "Thank you. He did scare me."

We began walking again.

"You know, Gildan, up until a few minutes ago I was afraid of you, too."

He laughed. "Fear is wasted on me. What is it? The eyes?" He was grinning.

I shook my head.

"No, it's not that. It's not what you look like. It's just that you're ..." it was my turn to search for the best word, "... so intense. It's like you're always carrying important things around in your head. You have to be so serious all the time."

He stopped walking again, considering what he had been told.

"You are right," he admitted. "I am ever the leader. I rarely think about anything other than what is best for Faerie."

He chuckled. "I do not believe I know how to be less than intense."

I squeezed his hand. "Faerie is lucky to have you. In my world, the leaders rarely care about the people like you do. All they care about is money and power and how to get more of both."

We reached the banks of the lake.

"So when are you going to tell me what you brought me out here to tell me?" I asked.

"Now who is the intense one?" He smiled. "Shall we sit for a moment?"

I made myself comfortable on a grassy spot along the lakeshore and gazed out across the water. A light wind riffled the surface. A fish jumped, snatched a low-flying insect, and vanished leaving behind only rings of ripples to mark its presence.

Gildan settled next to me with a grunt. A moment later I turned to speak to him and saw him holding a tiny mound of glitter in his palm.

"What's ..."

Before I could finish my question, he blew the glitter into my face. I gasped and choked, and he grabbed my arm before I could topple over.

"What are you – why – why ..." my voice faded and I sat quietly, my eyes open, in a trance.

"Odessa, you are safe and comfortable. You are not afraid. You are calm and relaxed."

Gildan spoke with authority and I believed him. I sat relaxed, looking at him with my muscles loose and no fear in my eyes. Despite our short acquaintance, I trusted him.

He took a small jar from his pocket and uncapped it.

"Listen to me, Odessa. Remember what I am going to tell you. The Faerie you see here now is not real. What you are seeing, instead, is Glamour. Faerie is suffering the same ill-effects on the environment as is your Earthly Realm. Faerie is a part of the Earth that Humans can no longer see, except for you. They do not realize that the damage done to Earth's environment also affects Faerie."

"I want you to see what has been done. I am going to lift the Glamour so that you can see the sickness for yourself. Will you allow me to do that? It will not harm you."

"Yes," I whispered. I was asleep but oddly aware. I could see Gildan and understand his words, but at the same time he was distant and blurry.

He dipped his index finger into the jar and applied a dab of thin ointment on each of my eyelids. Then he recapped the jar and returned it to his pocket. "Close your eyes," he instructed, and I obeyed.

"I hope I am doing the right thing," he said softly. "There is no guarantee that she will see Earth again, but if she does, this may be Faerie's only chance to get the message out."

Gildan shook away his unhappy thoughts and took a breath. "Now open your eyes, Odessa, and See."

I Saw – and it was horrible. The brownish water of ToadSpit Lake lapped weakly onto banks dotted with crumbling boulders. Where lily pads had bloomed lushly on the surface, they were now few and sickly-looking. The black willow trees were leafless and bark was peeling from their thin trunks. The bulrushes were gone and the wetland grasses were frail and broken. The feeble waves pushed an oily film onto the bank, which was dotted with small dead fish. The air reeked of rot and despair.

Gildan stood. "Come, Odessa. Walk with me."

I rose obediently and followed him back onto the path. As we passed through the Becharmed Forest, again I Saw.

Where live oak trees had stood for ages in regal splendor, they now sent out short, squatted branches that had broken off and littered the ground. They were gray, cadaverous ghosts, devoid of life. Strings of rotted Spanish moss hung limply on a few of the branches. The thickets, brush, and ferns were yellowish.

We walked on silently. There was no need for words. He stopped me as we reached Lull's cottage.

The stone cottage looked the same on the outside, but the scenery beyond did not. Agrarian Lea's wood and straw buildings were sagging and tired. Behind the village, desolate farmland was bordered with sparse hedges and dead shrubbery. Thin cows and horses searched ground barely prickled with edible grasses. The forest beyond was a meager shadow of itself. It no longer blanketed the base of the mountains. Instead, stark rock rose like unearthed bones.

I turned around to look at Gildan and received a dull shock. I was looking at a figure only three feet tall. He had been using Glamour to appear to be six feet tall.

"Please make it stop," I said. "I don't want to See any more."

Gildan walked me back to ToadSpit Lake. He sat on a boulder in front of me, one hand reaching into his pocket.

"Odessa, what you have seen and what I am about to tell you will live in your subconscious mind until you awake in your own bed back in the Earthly Realm. When you remember, you will communicate all that you have experienced in Faerie to as many people as you can. You will ask for help for Faerie. Do you understand?"

"Yes, I understand," I said quietly.

"All right. When I wake you, you will have no conscious memory of anything but having had a pleasant chat with me beside the lake."

He produced a soft cotton handkerchief from his pocket. Gildan gently removed the ointment from my eyelids before removing another tiny jar from his pocket. He placed a pinch of a different-colored dust on his palm. "Now close your eyes," he said, and he blew the dust from his hand into my face. As my eyes flew open, he offered his hand.

"Shall we go back now?" he asked. "Lull will throw a fuss at me if I keep you from your chores much longer."

I smiled and took his hand as I got to my feet. "This has been lovely. I feel like we're friends now."

I also felt something that I couldn't explain – as though I carried some special knowledge about him, about some vulnerability he had trusted to me somehow, but which I couldn't quite put my finger on.

He gave a slight bow. "That we are."

We walked back to the cottage where Lull proceeded to scold Gildan just as he had predicted she would. He cast a private wink at me before escaping the cottage.

Chapter 8
Humans in Faerie

Autumn in Agrarian Lea is a time of preparing food for the winter months ahead. Because I couldn't stand sitting around any longer waiting for the Silver Company to announce its decision about me, I threw off my deepening depression of the last couple of weeks and immersed myself in helping Lull with her farm work. Not only did it keep my mind off my predicament, but it also made me feel good about myself. The physical labor was good for both body and spirit.

At present, I was learning how to prepare beef quarters for salting and drying. We trimmed away fat, since lean meat was best for this procedure. Lull demonstrated (with one of her Dirk Tribe knives) how to cut the large muscles out and then split them evenly along the muscle fibers. It took me, however, quite a few tries to cut the strips into uniform slices. Unevenly cut meat would dry unevenly and could spoil.

While I was laboring over slicing the beef strips, Lull filled a cauldron with water and added the salt. She stirred for quite a while to thoroughly dissolve the salt crystals. We added the beef strips to the brine to soak.

"Let's you and I have a sip of tea and rest our weary selves," Lull suggested.

I smiled. "That's the best idea I've heard all day. I had no idea how exhausting this kind of work is. How in the world have you done it all by yourself?"

Lull poured tea. "Oh, I don't. I usually hire someone to help me. And, if he's not occupied elsewhere, Gildan will lend a hand."

"How long have you known him?"

"All of my life. I can't imagine Faerie without Gildan in it."

We sipped our tea for a few moments.

"Lull, what are you?" I asked on impulse, and then caught myself. "Oh, I'm sorry. That came out wrong. I mean, except for your pointed ears, you seem so Human to me that I sometimes forget you're Fey."

Lull tittered, but it seemed forced. "I'm of the Deer Tribe. It would be hard to run a farm with hooves instead of these." She waggled her thumbs.

Her face grew serious. "Don't let the 'round ears' nonsense you hear from Elves and others bother you. It's an old prejudice they just can't seem to let go of. I like your round ears just fine."

Lull smiled at me over the top of her teacup and I suddenly felt sad. I was growing very fond of this woman.

"I'm going to miss you when I go back home."

"No more than I'll miss you," Lull said as she placed her teacup on the counter. "Let's get back to work or we'll be slaving away after dark."

Hours later, when the last strip of beef was hung to dry, I cheered. Lull joined in, giggling. We danced for a moment in the dying light of the day, and then holding hands, retired to the cottage for some supper and sleep.

I was half-asleep on my feet, rinsing the supper dishes, when someone knocked on the door. Lull answered it and stood in the doorway for a moment, talking to the visitor. Then she stepped aside and allowed a woman to enter.

My first impression was of a Fae high school cheerleader. The woman was slender and blonde and wore a short white skirt with a shimmery silver blouse and knee-high white boots. Silver wings framed her figure and waist-length hair.

"Hello, I am Tempestra, Lady of the Sylphs. I am here to meet with you, Odessa Chase, on behalf of the Silver Company," she chirped with a bright smile.

I dried my hands, my stomach suddenly churning. Had the Company made their decision? I had expected Gildan to inform me of the news, not a stranger.

Lull saw my distress and took over. "Come, both of you, sit and I'll make tea."

"How can I help you?" I asked Tempestra once we were settled. I was surprised and embarrassed to hear my voice shaking.

Tempestra frowned. "Oh, dear, I seem to have upset you somehow." Then her pretty face brightened. "I am simply here to visit with you. The Company has made no decision yet."

I sat back, relieved and yet disappointed, too. I did want this situation to end, yet I felt conflicting emotions about it. I loved being on the farm with Lull, but I also wanted to go back home.

"When Lord Gildan spoke of you, I became curious. We have not had a Human here for at least three hundred years. I have forgotten what Humans are like, so I wanted to meet you before we make our decision. I realized that if you went right back to Earth, I would miss the opportunity to meet you. So, I am meeting you now."

I almost smiled. Tempestra's lilting voice reminded me of Glinda the Good Witch in *The Wizard of Oz*. It was easy to lose myself in the rhythm of her voice and not hear what was being said. I straightened my back and came to attention. "What would you like to know?"

"Lord Gildan told us that Humans have magic over communication. If we were to send you back to Earth, could you use that magic to tell others of your experiences here?"

She leaned forward. Her legs were crossed and the top foot bounced restlessly.

"Well, yes, I could."

Suspicious thoughts buzzed in my brain. *Why is she asking this? Will they keep me here to keep me from telling others? Or does it not matter to them?*

"But it's not magic, really," I said. "We have what are called cell phones. Everyone is assigned a number, and we use the cell phone to call that number. Then we talk to each other over the device."

"By 'everyone,' who do you mean?" Tempestra asked, looking confused. "Surely you cannot mean everyone on Earth."

"No, not everyone," I agreed. "But we can talk to anyone in the world who has a phone number."

Tempestra's expressive face showed astonishment. "And do you? Do you talk to all of those Humans?"

I laughed. "No, I talk to only a few people. People that I know. I just talk to my friends and a few business associates."

Lull returned to the room and served tea with ginger cookies.

"I really don't know that many people," I admitted. "I'm an artist and I work at home. Most of my friends have families so they're not able to socialize much. I spend a lot of time alone – but that's good for my art."

Tempestra smiled and nibbled daintily on a ginger cookie. "Are you an artist of influence?"

"Oh, no, I'm not at all famous. My work has started to be shown in a few exhibits, but so far I haven't even been able to make *Ceramics Monthly*. That's a magazine."

I finally decided to be forthright and end my suspense.

"These are strange questions. Why are you asking me about communication and how well I'm known? If you don't want me to tell anyone on Earth about Faerie, I won't."

Tempestra loosed an airy laugh and tossed her long hair over one shoulder. "Oh, I am simply curious about the Earthly Realm and how you fit into it. As I said before, it has been a long time since I have conversed with a Human. I do hope I have not offended you. Gildan tells me I should think more before I speak, but then, what do you expect of someone from the Land element?"

She giggled.

"I'm not offended."

I picked up a cookie and munched it nervously.

Tempestra set down her teacup and turned suddenly to Lull. "Do you happen to have any of that lovely carbonated water that Gildan brings from BacchusYard?"

Lull shook her head. "I must apologize, but I have none. Would you like more tea?"

"Oh no," Tempestra waved. "I was just hoping."

Tempestra turned her attention back to me.

"Do you have any questions of me?" she asked, tilting her head.

"Actually, I do," I said, putting down my cookie. "You mentioned that there have been Humans here before. Could you tell me about them? Did they like it here?"

Tempestra took a deep breath and exchanged a glance with Lull. "I have changed my mind. May I have a sip of tea, please?"

"Let me see … how do I explain this?" she mused, watching Lull pour. "You may have noticed that there are not a lot of children here. Perhaps because we are so long-lived, reproduction has been a problem for the Folk for as far back as we can remember." She wrinkled her pretty face into a frown.

"Except for the Goblins. For some reason, they can fill up a cave with babies in no time. They are so ugly I just cannot imagine what they see in each other, do you? But whatever it is, they have no problem making babies. Ugly babies." She wrinkled her nose. "I love babies, but Goblin babies?" She tittered.

"King Oberon tried to solve the problem by trading Goblin sucklings for Human infants. It is no wonder that Humans wanted to give them back!"

"Yes, I've read stories about changelings," I offered. "People would wake up to find that their babies had been switched during the night."

"Yes, and once in a while, one of those mothers would find her way here while searching for her child. King Finvarra decreed an experiment to have these Humans bear Folk young in order to keep the bloodlines going. But that did not help because the Humans were mortal and their genes weaker than the Goblins'. They could never make a pretty Goblin baby, so the experiments fell out of practice."

"It was one of those young women that I knew briefly in – oh my, was it that long ago? – 1705. She was one of the last to be brought here."

"What happened to her? Was she happy here?"

Tempestra sighed. "She died during a childbirth. It was such a shame. Her name was Elsabeth. She loved to sing and dance. We danced under many a full moon. She was beautiful – for a Human." She gasped at her gaffe and slapped a hand to her mouth.

I smiled. "It's all right. What happened to those Humans who didn't successfully mate with the Fae but lived?"

"Oh, they became servants or were used in the ..." she caught herself. "... were used to teach us about Humans," she finished quickly.

I realized that Lull was sitting very still and quiet beside me, which was unusual for her. Before I could say anything to her, Tempestra addressed me again.

"WintersFeast is coming up on the twenty-first of December. One thing the Company did want me to ask is that you be our guest for the celebration. Believe me, you will enjoy yourself. There is food and games and lots and lots of music and dancing. Are you at all interested?"

I couldn't help frowning. "That's two months away. I was hoping to be back home before then."

Lull leaned forward and clasped my hand. "Two months is not very long. I doubt that the Company will have reached a decision before then. But even if they do allow you to leave, surely you can stay with me – with us – that long?"

I couldn't resist Lull's pleading eyes. Impulsively I answered, "How can I say no to you?"

Lull laughed and hugged me, spilling her tea in the process.

"We'll have so much fun baking and sewing and getting ready," she enthused as she mopped up the spill with her apron.

Tempestra stood up, smiling. "Well, good. At least one decision has been made. It has been a pleasure visiting with you, but now I must go."

She turned to Lull. "The tea and cookies were delicious. I can hardly wait to sample what you bring to WintersFeast."

Then she looked at me. "I think your decision to stay until after WintersFeast will make everyone happy. I am certain that Lord Gildan will inform you of the Company's decision the moment it is made."

Lull and I walked Tempestra to the door and saw her off. I yawned as Lull closed the door.

"You poor thing. I've worked you too hard today. Go on to bed. I'll clean up."

For once I didn't argue. I was too tired to even question my spontaneous decision to attend WintersFeast before returning home, if the decision went my way. I stumbled to my room and fell onto my bed, not even bothering to undress. I was asleep almost as soon as I closed my eyes.

Within a few days I had fallen into a routine. Lull had assigned me various chores around the small farm, helping her with care of the livestock and preparing food for the coming winter.

My favorite chore was tending to the chickens every day. Lull's chickens were funny-looking and always made me smile. They looked like soft cotton balls on legs. A foamy tuft of feathers covered their heads and eyes in a chicken-afro. Only their beaks protruded from the fuzz.

Silky white feathers covered even their legs, and their tails were an explosion of feathers in the rough shape of a rabbit's tail. I'd never seen anything like them before, but immediately fell in love with them.

Feeding time became my favorite time of the morning as I threw crumble to them and watched them squabble over the pickings. Despite their being so similar in appearance, I was soon able to pick out individuals by their behavior.

One was a terrible flirt whenever the rooster was around. Another tended to avoid the company of the other hens and flapped her downy wings at me when she wanted more crumble. Some were the best of friends; others fought whenever they saw each other. I was amazed that so much personality resided in birds I had always thought to be stupid.

The other part of my job was to gather eggs each day. Each hen laid one or two eggs each day, usually no later than noon. At first I was worried about being pecked by the hens as they defended their nests, but Lull showed me that the nesting boxes had clever trap doors in the rear so I could reach the eggs without disturbing the broody hens.

Some of the eggs were kept for eating and the rest went to market. Whatever money I received for the eggs was mine to keep. My other chores were not paid, but were in trade for my housing.

The work was physical and the days were long. Only a few weeks had passed before I noticed that I was losing weight and becoming stronger and more toned from all the activity and healthy eating. My biggest surprise, though, was the discovery that I was the happiest I could ever remember feeling.

Gildan made a habit of stopping by the cottage every evening. Usually he and I would take a stroll and talk about whatever came up in conversation. On one such walk I questioned him about how I was able to understand the Fae and they understand me; not all of them could be speaking English. He explained that it was a form of Glamour that translated our speech for us. I never quite understood, but accepted his explanation.

On another walk we discussed Elves.

"Lull said something the other day about my keeping away from Elves if I see them, that they don't like Humans much. Why is that? Back home, Elves are always portrayed as friendly to Humans."

Gildan pursed his lips, then answered, "Elves and Humans did get along at first. You know that Elves are of the forests and are very protective of the woodlands. Once they saw the destruction of the forests in the Earthly Realm, they became resentful."

"I don't blame them for that," I mused, gazing at the Becharmed Forest around us. "Earth is in a very bad place right now. But why would the Elves feel so strongly about what happens on Earth?"

"You forget that Earth is our sister plane. The destruction there is echoed here. It is not as apparent to the eye here, but we are definitely affected. The plight of the Earth is exhausting Mother Nature. She is not able to give Faerie the attention it deserves. The Elves are angry about this injustice and blame the Humans. It is not fair, but emotions rarely are, especially passionate ones."

"Well, the Elves aren't the only resentful ones. I'm not very happy with my fellow Humans myself." I began to pace in front of him, listing items on my fingers. "I read recently that one-fourth of the Earth's animals are facing extinction. Our oceans have dead zones that are doubling every ten years. Half of our rain forests will be gone in twice that. The polar ice caps are melting. And maybe worst of all, we're birthing millions of people every year who need all the resources that we're so quickly destroying."

I stopped walking and looked at him in the growing dusk. "Sorry for the rant, Gildan, but I don't know what the answer is, and it scares me to death. I feel so helpless about it."

Gildan nodded. "There is only so much one person can do besides enlisting the help of as many people as possible. The more minds working on a problem, the better the odds of reaching a solution."

"I'm doing what I can to spread the message. I do environmental art and support environmental causes. I just wish there was more I could do."

Gildan looped my arm through his and patted my hand. "I am sure the time will come when you will think of ways to help, things that are just lurking in your subconscious right now."

I looked up at him, taking comfort in his kindly face. "You talk as though I'll be going back."

"Do you still wish to return to Earth?" he asked. There was a careful lack of inflection in his voice.

I sighed, thinking for a moment. "As much as I like it here, yes, I still want to go back home."

Impulsively, I stepped up on my tiptoes and kissed his cheek. "I will miss you, though."

He looked down at me with a moment of surprise on his face. Then he kissed my forehead. "I will miss you, too, Odessa. But if Earth is where you want to be, I will do my best to see that you get there."

We walked back to the cottage. I felt a mixture of sadness that I would be leaving Lull and Gildan, but also a measure of relief at the idea of being back in my own comfortable world ... if the Company decided that I could leave, that is.

The next morning, Lull was like a whirlwind. She chatted nonstop during breakfast and rushed through the cleanup. Then she settled me at the table and we began to compile a list of the foodstuffs we would need to prepare for WintersFeast. Lull read through the recipes and I recorded the ingredients to be purchased.

Lull looked at the menu. "Roasted goose, garlic-infused lamb, fruited bread pudding, gingerbread cookies, apple pie, roasted bittersweet potatoes with pecans, pumpkin bread, and …" she looked up at me and grinned, "… Lull's Nutcake."

"From the smile on your face, I take it your nutcake is special," I teased.

"Oh, it is," Lull promised. "Come, let me show you my secret ingredient."

I followed Lull to her fruit cellar. There were rows of wood shelves containing baskets of vegetables, burlap sacks of grains, dried meats, flour, and jars of canned food. Lull went to one of the shelves and reached behind the canning jars. She pulled out a bottle of amber liquid.

"What is that?"

"Apple Brandywine," Lull said. "I use it for cooking, though I have been known to sneak a sip or two on a cold winter's night."

I smiled. "Where do you get it? I didn't see anything like that at the market."

"Oh, you haven't seen the whole of the market. But I get this from Gildan when he travels across the mountains to BacchusYard on Company business. This isn't sold at market here. It's available only from Bacchus, and that's quite a trek from here, so I guard my supply."

Lull shook an index finger at me. "You're sworn to secrecy, young lady. No one knows of my secret ingredient – and a few have been hungering to find out for years!"

"I promise," I replied. "Wild horses couldn't drag it out of me."

Lull returned the bottle to its hiding place, then turned and clapped her hands. "Let's go try on your WintersFeast dress. I want to make some adjustments."

I stood in the middle of the room while Lull arranged the pieces of my soon-to-be dress. She chattered non-stop as she worked.

"Lull," I interrupted. "You're so excited you're making me nervous." I laughed.

"I can't help myself! It's been so long since I've had a companion. I hadn't realized how much I've missed having someone around."

"Don't you have family?"

Lull shook her head. "No, my mother died 300 years ago and I am her only child."

I was shocked. "I thought the Fae were immortal!"

"No, not immortal, only long-lived. At 300 I'm middle-aged. I expect to live at least 400 years yet."

"You've never married?"

Lull busied herself with needle and thread. "No, as a younger woman I was too busy as a nursemaid to think about marriage."

"That fits you – being a nursemaid, I mean. I bet the children adored you."

Lull laughed. "Oh, I didn't nursemaid only children. I was a companion for the Humans who came to Faerie but didn't stay here." She winked at me. "I seem to have taken up my old occupation again."

"Well, any Human to have you as a companion is lucky," I declared. "I don't know what I would have done without you! When I woke up here, I was scared to death of Gildan – and you were so kind, you kept me from falling apart. I can't thank you enough for that, Lull."

"Your companionship is thanks enough," Lull assured me. "Now stand still while I piece this."

I was silent for a while, watching Lull work. Finally, curiosity forced me to speak.

"If you took care of Humans, then you must have known Elsabeth, too."

"In a way," Lull said, not looking at me.

"She was brought here specifically to have children?"

"Yes, she was."

"Was she happy here?"

Lull stopped working and sat heavily on the floor.

"No, not at first. She hadn't come here willingly, and it wasn't her choice to become pregnant."

Lull looked sad as she revisited the memories. "She was a virgin when she came to Faerie. She fought her role here. It was very hard for her. She was a sweet young woman when she wasn't battling her servitude."

"That's horrible!" I cried. "How could you just stand by and allow that?"

Lull shook her head. "I was not involved. Elsabeth was courted by those the King deemed suitable, but she was young and headstrong. She refused to accept a husband, no matter what they offered her. In the end, she was taken by the King.

He wasn't a bad man, but also not a particularly understanding one. He forced her into pregnancy. Over time, Elsabeth seemed to adjust to her life, and she was actually happy and excited about her pregnancy. When she died in childbirth, it was a tremendous loss for me. You see, Elsabeth was my mother."

I gasped, shook off the piecemeal garment, and knelt to hug her. "I'm so sorry! That explains where your Human side came from. Thank you for telling me."

Lull sniffled and wiped away her tears with her apron. "I'm just being a silly old woman. Back to work with us!"

Chapter 9
The Vote

Poseida, Tempestra, and even the accidentally-on-purpose tardy Adram were waiting for him when Gildan entered the Company courtyard. This was a closed meeting.

Adram held a glass of beer and stared moodily into the distance as the two women talked quietly. Adram roused himself and saluted Gildan with the half-full glass as he approached. "It is a fine day for a sip."

Gildan took his place at the table as a servant appeared with a tea tray.

"Spirits are for celebrations, are they not? What are you celebrating?" Gildan asked as he prepared his tea with cream and sugar.

Adram threw him a coy look. "Oh, nothing in particular."

Gildan stirred the tea and took a sip, ignoring Adram's attempt to engage more questions.

"Shall we begin?" Poseida asked. "I am eager for this matter to be settled."

Adram sat back in his chair and nursed his beer.

"As am I," Gildan agreed. "Lady Tempestra, I believe when we last met you planned to visit with Odessa before making your decision."

Tempestra nodded. "Yes, I did meet with her. She is quite nice, and Lull appears to adore her." She paused, looking troubled. "I wish I could tell you that I was impressed with what she had to say. However, when I questioned her, she informed me that she does not have any influence in the Earthly Realm. She also does not know many other Humans. How can she spread your message if this is so?"

"She has Human technological magic at her disposal," he replied.

"True, but what good is that if she has no one to share her magic with?"

Adram jumped in. "And even if she did tell the whole of the Earthly Realm, how many would believe her? More important, what could they actually do about it if they did believe her? Who is to say there is anything the Humans can do? Their magic concerns machines, not Nature."

"You make good points," Gildan admitted. "However, if there is but a small chance of success, I believe we should make the attempt."

Adram snorted. "I do not understand why there is a problem! One, we have no need of her here. She is too old to bear children. Two, she is already here in time for WintersFeast. And three, we need not sacrifice another Fae since she is available. My Fire Folk are demanding that we offer her to The Huntress."

"There would be no 'demand' had you not inflamed their passion, Lord Adram," Gildan flicked an angry glance at him.

"Be that as it may, their wishes are clear." Adram shrugged and smirked.

Gildan looked at Poseida. "You have been very quiet in this matter, Lady Poseida. What is the opinion of the Undines?"

Poseida met his silver eyes with her sea-green gaze. "The Undines are in favor of a Human Hunt," she said quietly. "It is not my personal choice, but as Lord Adram has pointed out, I must act in favor with the wants of my people. Since most of the Undines are Huntresses by nature, the last 300 years has been hard for them. They are eager to return to their old ways."

There was a giggle. It was Tempestra, and she was rubbing her nose. "The bubbles tickle," she explained, and then returned her carbonated water to the table.

She looked at Gildan, suddenly as serious as she had been silly.

"I realize that you believe you can save Faerie. For some reason I cannot fathom, you have taken the weight of Faerie on your shoulders from the day you became a Lord. Has it never occurred to you, Good Sir, that for all your good intentions, you may never claim success? Faerie's problems are simply too huge for one man to handle."

"I must agree with her," Poseida spoke up. "Do you not find it strange that the Earthly Realm has not solved their environmental problems on their own? Why is it you believe they can save us when they cannot save themselves?"

"Like I said, who cares if the message gets sent to everyone on Earth if none of them give a damn? Obviously they don't, or they would be busy saving Earth," Adram agreed. "I say we vote. We are wasting time with this chatter."

Gildan sighed. "How vote you, Lady Poseida?"

"Aye for the Human Hunt."

"How vote you, Lady Tempestra?"

"Aye for the Human Hunt."

"How vote you, Lord Adram?"

"Aye for the Human Hunt!"

"I vote nay for the Human Hunt." Gildan looked at each of them. "I concede my loss."

Adram leaped to his feet. "Shall we call for a round of beer to celebrate the return of the Old Ways?"

"None for me," Gildan said as he rose slowly, like a much older man. "I do not feel like celebrating."

He took a deep breath as though preparing to shout, but then said calmly, "Good afternoon, Ladies and Lord."

Gildan had walked barely half the length of the courtyard when two puffs of smoke exploded on either side of him. The displaced air was filled with two smoky figures that emerged from the cloudy wisps of smoke. The ruddy-skinned, bald humanoids with lightning crackling in their eyes each grabbed one of Gildan's arms.

"Adram!" Gildan cried, looking back over his shoulder. "What are you doing?"

"My best, Lord G.," Adram sneered, and saluted him once more. "Some of my best work."

There was only time for Gildan to notice Poseida sobbing salty tears that left brine behind on her lovely face before the Djinn vanished, taking Gildan with them.

"Oh, for the Gods' sake, Poseida!" Adram snarled. "He will come to no harm. I am merely making sure that the Good Sir does not warn the Human before the Hunt. Stop sniveling!"

Poseida turned wet eyes that mirrored a stormy sea on him.

"You had best see to it that Lord Gildan returns in good health," she replied in a low, menacing voice. "You know what happens when fire meets water."

Adram rolled his eyes and drained his glass. There was just a tiny tremor to his grip as he returned the glass to the table.

Chapter 10
WintersFeast

ull and I stood close to the crackling fires that burned in the oven pits, enjoying the warmth as the autumn day chilled fingers and toes. We were in the garden behind her cottage, tending to the three pit ovens we had built in anticipation for WintersFeast.

A week earlier, we had dug three pits about a yard wide and a foot deep, which we then lined with rocks. We had gathered fire-making materials and arranged them in the pits before collecting three cowhides and large branches long enough to span the pits.

The plan was to wrap the food in leaves or wet cloths and allow the heat from the stones to cook the food after covering the pits with the branches and cowhides. We were now waiting for the fires to heat the stones to cooking temperatures.

"What does WintersFeast actually celebrate? I would think that winter is the hardest time of the year for farmers. What is there to celebrate?"

"It celebrates life in the face of death," Lull replied. "Winter is death, as is the Huntress. She hunts every 100 years – or used to, that is. She still appears every 100 years."

"Oh. I guess I'm lucky to be here at a time when I can see her, then."

Lull nodded, not meeting my eyes. She pushed her hands into her apron pockets and studied the slowly dying flames.

"The Hunt was brought here by the Huntress many, many centuries ago. It is – was – a barbaric thing before Faerie made it a celebration instead of something to be dreaded."

I looked at her with wide eyes. "The Wild Hunt? Is that what you mean?"

Lull started and returned wide eyes. "Lamb's ass, you've heard of it?"

"Well, yeah. I've read about it. It's a group of ghost riders led by a god or goddess, depending on the legend's origin."

"It's not a legend here."

"Lull, are you telling me that there really is a Wild Hunt? Someone is chased and killed?"

Lull's laugh was forced. "Not anymore. You see, the Huntress' preferred prey was Humans. It is believed that she accidentally entered Faerie while chasing a Human and now she and her horde are trapped here. There haven't been any Humans here for a long, long time, so the Hunt has become symbolic."

A sliver of fear pierced my chest and I shivered. "But I'm Human."

Lull pulled me into such an abrupt and violent embrace that I almost lost my footing.

"Don't you worry, Odessa. Nothing will happen to you," she said fiercely. "Gildan and I will see to that."

I hugged her back. "I know," I said into her ear.

She released me and we walked back to the cottage. Lull bustled around the kitchen, preparing tea and cookies. As she brought the tray bearing the treats to the table, I noticed a barely perceptible tremble before the tray met the table.

I twirled in my black ballgown and admired how the long skirt flowed loosely around my legs. It was long-sleeved, with an empire cut. As Lull had predicted, the silver threads embedded throughout the embroidery twinkled like tiny stars as they caught the light.

Because the nights were growing colder, Lull had added to her creation with a black velvet cape the same length as the dress. It had a hood, collar, and trim along the edges from the leftover dress material and was lined with black satin. Soft leather pointed-toed shoes laced around my ankles.

Lull was wearing a maroon velvet gown, also empire-waisted, with large puffy sleeves and a triangle of white velvet underskirt that showed in the front. A matching cape and white leather shoes completed her outfit. I had helped her pin her long braids into a bun on the back of her head, clipped with her rhinestone barrettes.

"You look lovely, Lull."

Lull ducked her head and grinned. "Not so bad for a nursemaid."

I laughed. "No one will think you a nursemaid tonight. You look like royalty. Men will be falling all over themselves to steal a dance with you."

"Oh, stop!" Lull protested, but I could tell she was secretly pleased. "You, Miss Odessa, now you are a vision in that dress."

"You know, I had my doubts about wearing a black dress, but as usual, you were right. I absolutely love it, and I can't thank you enough for making it for me. I've never had anything that fit so perfectly!"

"Aww, you know I enjoyed every moment. It was no trouble at all."

"I do wish Gildan was coming with us. I hate that he can't be here."

"Me, too," Lull replied. "I'm a bit surprised, actually, that he was called away to BacchusYard of all places. The Fauns do love festivals and have always attended WintersFeast before now. Whatever is keeping them and Gildan occupied must be very important. Usually Gildan tells me in person when he is called away. This is the first time he just left a note. Oh well." Lull took my arm. "I do believe it's time to go."

I opened the door and we stepped out. I clasped my cape against a chilly wind as we climbed into the wagon and settled ourselves on the seat.

"I'm glad I'm here for this," I said as we adjusted a wool blanket over our legs for the open-air ride. "I have the feeling this will be an unforgettable night."

Lull and I drove to Agrarian Lea and left the wagon in a field with many other wagons just outside of the town square. We could hear laughter, shouts, music, and song as we walked to the afternoon part of the festival in the square.

In a field adjacent to the parked wagons, Fae were taking turns at a crossbow shoot, competing to win prizes donated by the festival vendors. There was also a throwing game. A Fae thrust his garishly painted face through a hole in a wooden wall and dared passersby to hit him with raw eggs. We ignored his insults and passed into the square.

It looked similar to the weekly market but on a grander scale. Some tents housed games such as darts, dice, wheels, or fishing. Others sold cider and ale. Handcrafted items from plates to jewelry to winter clothing were emblazoned with the silhouette of a horned female figure, which for some reason I couldn't name, seemed creepy to me.

The festival attendees were wearing their finest formal attire and made striking figures. There was a riot of asymmetrical hems, hooped skirts both above the knee and below, and soft flowing fabrics trailing moving figures. Many of them reminded me of runway models at their most exotic.

As Lull and I entered the fray, I caught sight of some dolls for sale and stopped to look. They were all of the same female figure that was featured on the items I'd seen earlier. She wore a brown tunic and pants under a black cloak. Long black hair brushed her shoulders. A crescent moon tiara crowned her head. She held a bow in one hand, an arrow in the other.

"Who is this character?" I asked Lull. "Is she the goddess of WintersFeast?"

Lull looked at the doll in my hand. "That's the Goddess of the Hunt, the Huntress. See the tiara? The moon symbolizes horns. She's the personification of the wilderness." She took the doll from me. "It's nothing you need to worry about. Come, I see some entertainment over there. The dog show is about to begin."

I followed her to a space that had been set up for the performing dogs. The trainer wore a colorful costume of white pants that ballooned at the thigh, a red jacket with tails, and knee-high black boots. Her long black hair hung loose around her shoulders. The dogs were performing tricks, but it wasn't the tricks that had me mesmerized. Each of the dogs had a glossy, feline-patterned coat.

Lull pulled me to the front of the audience and we cheered as an orange, black-striped tiger-dog walked a tightrope. Then a tawny, heavy-maned lion-dog caught flying discs in mid-air. A tall black-and-white dog with a tuxedo-patterned coat made me think of my little friend Milk Monster back home, and for a moment I wondered if I'd see her again – here or in the Earthly Realm.

Two sleek, black Anubis-dogs with tall pointed ears and big golden eyes took turns leaping onto the back of a pony as it trotted in a circle. A yellow dog with black leopard spots climbed a rope ladder.

As one of the Anubis-dogs jumped to the ground from the pony's back, it suddenly stopped in its tracks. It scented the air, then stared at me. I noticed it just as its yellow eyes turned a bright, alarming red and it bared its teeth at me. It began a low, predatory stalk toward me.

I tried to back away, but the press of people around me left nowhere for me to go. Lull caught sight of what was happening and screamed. I turned back just as the animal leapt at me.

From out of the crowd, a large, heavily-muscled man stepped between me and the attacking dog. His big hands plucked the dog out of mid-air and snapped its neck with an audible crack of bone. He dropped the carcass, ignoring the cries of the dog trainer.

"Are you all right?" he asked me in a deep, hoarse voice.

I nodded from Lull's protective embrace.

"You killed Osiris!" the dog trainer screamed as she stood over the dog's body. "You killed my dog!"

The big man looked down at the dead animal and then back at the hysterical trainer.

"I had no choice. I could not allow it to harm the Human." He pointed at me. "Her safety comes before an animal's."

The trainer nodded, still sobbing. "I do not understand why Osiris did that. He has never done anything like that before."

I pulled out of Lull's grasp. "Thank you for saving me. Who are you?"

"Gid," he replied. "I have been sent to protect you."

I blinked with surprise as the broad-chested, strong-armed man with a tight ponytail stepped closer to us.

"Sent by whom? Protect me from what?" I asked, glancing at Lull. She shook her head and widened her eyes, indicating confusion.

"You were not to have seen me. Lord Gildan hired me to watch over you during all of WintersFeast."

"Gildan did? But why?" I persisted with impatience.

"He did not say there was a threat. Only that I am to watch you until he returns."

"I'm sure Gildan is over-reacting," Lull said. "WintersFeast gets rowdy once the ale and beer flow, but no one has ever come to serious harm. He's probably just nervous because he can't be here himself."

The dog trainer lifted the body of Osiris and carried him away. I turned to Gid, but he had melted into the crowd and was gone.

I sighed. "Let's go do something fun," I suggested. "I'm going to let Gid do the worrying for the rest of the night."

"I like the sound of that. Things have been too serious. Tonight we devote to free spirit!" Lull grinned. "I know just the thing that will cheer us and bore Gid to tears. Dancing shoes! We simply must have dancing shoes for tonight's revelry!"

I grinned back. "I've always been a sucker for shoes."

I tried on my fifth pair of shoes. So far I had tested strappy leather sandals, a pair of soft suede low-heeled short boots, and hard leather clogs, and was now working a pair of dress shoes onto my feet.

"What do you think?" I stood up, presenting one foot, then the other for Lull's opinion.

I tried to ignore the curious stare of the Elven shoe seller. All afternoon I had caught various Fae pointing or staring at me as Lull and I wended our way through the festival. I attributed it to being the only Human in Faerie and therefore a novelty, but it still made me uncomfortable. And this Elf wasn't even trying to hide her interest.

"They're nice," said Lull. "Can you dance in them?"

"Oh, that doesn't matter," I laughed. "I don't dance."

"Oh, dance you will," she assured me. "Once the music starts, everyone dances."

"I don't know how!" I insisted, wishing the subject dropped.

"Knowing how isn't what's important," Lull argued. "No one will be standing about pointing and saying, 'Look how badly the Human dances!' They will be too busy dancing themselves."

The Elf vendor reacted to the word "dance." She was a bright-eyed, green-haired young woman, wearing the native uniform of green tunic over green leggings and shoes with points that curled over her toes. She walked over to a table in the back and began searching the boxes stored underneath.

I returned the dress shoes to the table.

"I can't find anything anyway," I said as I gave up rummaging through the shoe displays.

"Perhaps you will fancy these," the Elf suggested.

I turned to see the vendor holding a pair of black shoes toward me. They were flats with a strap across the instep and another around the ankle. The shoes glinted with inset onyx gemstones.

"These were made for dancing," the young woman smiled.

"Thank you." I took the shoes. They would look nice with my dress. I sat down and started to put one on.

"NO!" Lull cried, running to me. She snatched the shoe out of my hands.

"Where did you get these?"

"From – from the seller," I answered, a bit bewildered by her reaction.

Lull whirled furiously toward the Elf. "How dare you!" she spat. She threw the shoe in her hand at the Elf, but missed.

The Elf stood with her head down, making no attempt to defend herself.

"How dare you try to trick her with those? Do you have no brain in your head?" Lull pulled me to my feet. "Come. We're leaving!"

As we moved to the tent opening, Lull hissed over her shoulder, "Expect to hear from Lord Gildan about this!"

The Elf flinched but did not look up. Lull stalked out of the tent, dragging me by the arm.

"Lull, stop! What's wrong?" I asked, hopping as I tried to put my own shoe back on.

"I should have expected something like this," Lull muttered. She shook her head, then stopped her outraged march. "Some people are just … puttocks!"

"Tell me what happened!" I demanded, starting to become angry myself.

Lull blew out a sigh. "Those were the Prancing Shoes." She closed her eyes, taking a moment to calm herself. "Anyone who wears them dances until they die of exhaustion. The Elves used to entertain themselves by gifting them to Humans and watching them dance themselves to death."

"Surely the vendor didn't know what they were," I objected.

"Oh, she knew," Lull contradicted, her voice bitter. "She couldn't keep herself from trying to harm you because you're Human." She glared back at the tent. "Perhaps Gildan was right to assign you a protector."

I tried to smile, but it fell flat. "I've never been a victim of bigotry before."

"Well, such a thing won't happen again in my presence."

Just then there came the sound of shrieks and thumps from inside the shoe tent. There was a loud ripping sound and we looked back to see passersby fleeing and the shoe vendor's ripped tent billowing. A display table flew through the opening to crash onto the ground. The Elf came running out, followed by a rain of shoes.

Neither Lull nor I were surprised to see Gid emerge from the damaged tent with an armful of boxes. "Shoes for the taking!" he bellowed, throwing the boxes at surprised spectators. The Elf tried to keep an eye on him and pick up shoes at the same time.

"Well," I said, "at least we know for sure he's watching."

With a satisfied smile, Lull took my arm and we resumed strolling the festival.

A bell rang out from the tower atop the Banquet Hall. Lull and I joined the lines of Fae entering the building through its four double-doors. Inside, tables draped with silver and white tablecloths lined three walls of the huge room. I was stunned at the array of foods displayed – there was an orgy of roasted nuts, leaf salads, eggs for sucking, parsley soup, and saffron bread. Tables were loaded with Paprika Rabbit, Roasted Bittersweet Bugbear, Apple and Lavender Fish, Mustard and Thyme Lamb, Ginger Frog, Venison with Acorn Noodles, Tea-smoked Mushrooms, Honey and Nut Potatoes, Onion and Cream Winter Vegetables, and a multitude of other dishes I couldn't begin to identify.

It took two tables to hold the honey cakes, chestnut pudding, plum doughnuts, fruited cookies, nectar-infused fruit, and a huge variety of candies and tarts.

The rest of the dining room was filled with round tables and chairs. Each table featured an ice sculpture as a centerpiece. Some were elaborate abstracts; others were realistic renditions of animals.

At the very back wall above the food tables was a raised stage upon which the musicians performed. Wearing brightly colored outfits of red and gold, they played recorders with different voices in unison. The music could barely be heard over the thunder of so many voices. I was sure that once all those mouths were busy with the food, I would be able to enjoy the music.

There were so many people in attendance that it took a while for Lull and me to fill our plates and find seats. We sat at a table with several Fae already in place. One was a very handsome black-haired, blue-eyed Butterfly Fae. His wings were bright blue, trimmed in black, and matched his formal clothing.

Next to him were two women who appeared Human except for their pointed ears. Their similarity of features made it obvious that they were mother and daughter. The mother was white-haired and wrinkled and appeared a bit frail. Her green satin dress seemed a little bit young for her. The daughter was busy cutting something on her mother's plate and didn't look up as Lull and I sat down.

Next to them were two Sylphs wearing fluttery, fussy white clothing. One male, one female, their transparent wings trembled with excitement as they took turns flirting with the Butterfly Fae.

Lull suddenly froze with her fork halfway to her mouth. She was staring at two Fauns who had just passed the table. One was taller and older and wore a wine-red tunic with the insignia of a cluster of grapes. The bottom half of his body was hairy and unclothed. Following behind him was a younger, good-looking subservient male wearing a purple tunic.

"What's the matter?" I asked.

Lull pointed with her fork. "The one in the red is the Bacchus councilman. He's the one Gildan is supposed to be meeting with. Why is he here and Gildan isn't?"

I shrugged. "Perhaps Gildan was delayed and will be here later. I hope so."

Lull nodded. "You're probably right." She resumed eating, but her expression remained suspicious.

I looked up from my plate to find the old woman with pointed ears staring at me. I smiled at her and reached for my glass.

"Are you a Human?" the old woman asked in a tremulous voice.

"Yes, I am."

"What's that again?" the old woman asked loudly.

"Yes, yes, I'm Human," I repeated.

"Speak up, young woman. Don't mumble!"

The daughter leaned toward her mother and shouted in her ear, "She's Human, Mother!"

"I thought so. Those round ears are a give-away." The old woman chuckled to herself. "Round-Ears, Round-Ears."

The daughter shrugged an apology and I smiled at her.

"When I was young, calling someone a round-ears was fighting words!" the old woman declared, turning spiteful eyes on me. "You want to fight me, Round-Ears?"

"Mother! Stop it!" the daughter yelled in her mother's ear. She turned to me. "I am sorry. She just gets ornery sometimes."

"It's all right," I said, trying hard not to get angry with the old woman. She obviously wasn't in her right mind and shouldn't be blamed for her crass behavior.

"It is not all right," Lull objected, pointing her fork at the old woman. "Can you not control your mother?"

The daughter shot Lull an angry glare. "She means no harm. She is old and senile."

The old woman ate a couple more bites, oblivious to the conversation about her. She glanced at her daughter sideways, then sat grasping her fork. "You here for the Hunt, Round-Ears?"

Everyone at the table froze and stared at her except for me. I replied, "No, ma'am, I'm here for WintersFeast."

The old woman stared at me intently, reading my lips. "Hah!" she spat, "the Hunt *is* WintersFeast. It's the best part!"

"Mother, stop it this instant or I will take you home!" The daughter was close to tears from embarrassment.

The old woman sat back in her chair, grinning. Everyone else at the table resumed talking and eating. "Round-Ears, Round-Ears, this is the night of the Round-Ears," she crooned to herself, darting sly looks between me and her daughter.

A short while later the daughter coaxed the old woman out of her chair to go look at the dessert table. I was relieved to see them go. Lull chattered merrily with everyone else at the table.

Eventually the Bell Tower sounded a series of chimes.

"Ahhh!" Lull gave a happy cry. "It's time to dance!"

The Grand Ballroom was even larger than the Banquet Hall, and looked like something out of a dream. The walls were opaque glass with "fairy lights" illuminating them from behind. White marble columns framed each glass panel. From the center of the white-on-white carved ceiling hung a massive chandelier, also glass, with thousands of candle flames reflecting in the cut glass.

Musicians in formal attire sat on a raised platform at the end of the room. They held recorders, flutes, drums, whistles, Pan pipes, and strangely S-curved horns. A harpist sat to one side.

I looked around for a place to sit and watch, but there was no seating provided. I leaned against a wall and prayed I would not be asked to dance. I had always meant to take dancing lessons, but never seemed to get around to it.

Lull stood beside me, literally twitching with excitement. She looked so lovely in her maroon gown and sparkly barrettes.

A man strode out onto the platform and stood in front of the musicians. He wore an ice-blue suit with a crisp white shirt. Holding a hand up for quiet, he waited until he had the attention of the crowd.

"Good evening, everyone. I am Jasper Reeve, speaking for Lord Gildan who cannot be with us tonight. It is my pleasure to welcome you to this year's WintersFeast. WintersFeast is a grand tradition that the Folk have been celebrating since time immemorial. This is a time of welcoming Winter, the Season of Death. It is a time of rest from the labors of Spring planting and Fall harvest. It is a time of cold and darkness that we suffer before the return of the Light."

"Each WintersFeast features a Wild Hunt to symbolize the coming of the Season of Death. Before we enjoy that spectacle, it is time to celebrate life. I now release you to dance and make merry! Happy WintersFeast to you all!"

The musicians began to play, and within moments the ballroom floor was filled with dancers. Ballgowns of every color shone in the fairy lights, contrasting against dark formal clothing. The dancers floated gracefully, their liquid movements mimicking the wind among leaves.

I smiled as I watched a middle-aged Elf approach Lull and ask her to dance. She giggled and took his hand. He escorted her to the floor and they were soon lost among the whirling figures.

As the music played, the pipes sweet, the drums a soft heartbeat, I found my foot moving in rhythm. The urge moved slowly up my legs, making it hard to stand still and hug the wall. Before I quite knew how it had happened, I was on the dance floor, alone, swaying and stepping in instinctual, primal movements I hadn't realized I knew.

It felt wonderful to surrender and allow the music to instruct my body. I twirled, laughing, and danced the dance of my moon-worshiping ancestors, pagan women experiencing freedom and delight and the magic of moonlight.

When the music stopped, my trance slowly melted. I saw Lull and her companion and started toward them, only to be stopped by the Butterfly Fae who had shared my dinner table.

"Will you dance with me?" he asked politely.

I shook my head. "I'm sorry. I don't dance well."

"You were doing well just a few moments ago." He held out his hand in invitation.

As if in a dream, I accepted his hand, and we danced. I forgot my fear and forgot where I was. I forgot about everything but the sound of the music. I followed the Fae's cues without thinking. Once again, not knowing how I knew, I danced.

I danced that night like I had never danced before. I danced alone and with partners. I danced until I was exhausted. The music stopped, and finally, finally, the music's spell lifted.

I made my way back to the edge of the dance floor, looking for Lull. Everyone was leaving the floor around me, making it hard to see. As the floor emptied, though, movement caught my eye.

A lone woman was still dancing despite the lack of music. She was moving erratically, as though she had lost control of her body. When I caught a glimpse of her terrified face, I realized that she was the daughter of the senile old woman.

A cluster of laughing Elves watched the woman dance. They wore tunics and matching leggings of brown or green. Their green hair fell down their backs in coarse needles that resembled porcupine quills, and rattled with their laughter.

The woman danced past me again, and one of her black shoes, studded with onyx stones, kicked out from beneath her skirt. I recognized the Prancing Shoes and gasped. She looked around for help as the shoes forced her around the floor, but the surrounding

110

Fae were either watching her and laughing or ignoring her plight altogether. Angry now, I marched out onto the floor and grabbed the woman's arm.

"Leave her be, Round-Ears!" called one of the Elves. "This is none of your concern!"

The woman couldn't stand still and dragged me with her as she continued to writhe in her music-less dance. I hooked a foot behind the woman's legs and knocked her down. As angry Elves charged onto the floor, I managed to pull one shoe from the woman's foot.

The Elves grabbed hold of my arms and lifted me away from her. I struggled against them. "Let me go! This is cruel! How can you just stand and watch this?"

"Stay out of this, Human!" a voice spat in my ear. I was shoved away. I lost my balance and fell at the feet of the ring of spectators.

It took me a moment to regain my stunned senses. Through the forest of Elven tights, I saw the woman still on the floor, being jerked spasmodically by the remaining Prancing Shoe on her foot. The Elves were hooting and laughing.

Thoroughly enraged now, I scrambled to my feet and charged at the Elves' backs. I knocked them aside and fell onto the woman's legs, trapping her long enough to rip the remaining shoe from her foot. Gasping for air, the woman lay on the floor, her over-worked muscles trembling from head to toe.

"How dare you!?" I screamed, nearly out of my mind with fury. I threw the Prancing Shoe and hit one of the Elves in the chest. "If this is so funny, you wear the goddamned shoes!"

Grimacing with anger, the Elf scooped the shoe up from the floor and stalked toward me. "I believe it is your turn, Round-Ears."

I scrabbled backward, finding it hard to gain traction on the slick dance floor. Then, it seemed, everything happened at once.

"Stop!" bellowed a voice. The onlookers parted to reveal Gid plowing his way through the crowd.

The Elf with the shoe stopped to look at Gid. I took that moment to regain my footing. As I stood up, the Elf gestured to his peers. All together, they turned their backs and their hair-quills began to rise.

"They're going to shoot!" someone cried, and the spectators began running in all directions.

I turned to run as Gid hurled himself at me and took me to the floor. The air bristled with green quills that shot over and past us as we slid across the floor into the wall. There were cries of pain as those accidently shot began pulling at the quills in their bodies.

"Enough! Elves stand down!"

This order came from a different voice. The Elf that had been dancing with Lull all evening was now confronting his peers. "I will not have this at WintersFeast!"

The Elf holding the Prancing Shoe stepped forward. The other Elves melted into the background.

"The Human is at fault. She had no right to interfere."

"I do not care who is at fault, Donnglen. I will not stand for violence at a festival. If you or any of the other soldiers are involved in any more trouble, you will never see another WintersFeast. Is that understood?"

Donnglen nodded. He dropped the shoe and kicked it away. Then with head held high, he walked away.

Gid climbed off me. "Are you all right?"

I nodded. "I'll have some bruises tomorrow, but I'm all right."

"Odessa! Odessa!" Lull came across the hall at a run. She fell to her knees beside me as I sat on the floor, testing my ankles. "Are you all right? I thought the Elves had shot you!"

"I'm fine. Gid pushed me out of the way."

I turned to thank him, but once again he had vanished.

Lull helped me to my feet. Around us, the Fae were staring and talking in excited but low voices. When Lull and I reached the outskirts of the dance floor, the older Elf was waiting.

"I must apologize for my soldiers," he said. "They will face discipline for their actions tonight."

The host of the dance, Jasper Reeve, appeared and ushered Lull and me to a corner of the room where two chairs and a small table had been set up for us. On the table was a tea service. "Please," he invited us, "take a few moments to rest."

"Thank you," I answered, slumping into one of the chairs. "I'm sorry for causing a disruption."

"Not at all," he assured me, and then hurried away.

"Lull, I don't know what happened," I said as she poured tea. "When I saw how they were laughing at that woman, I just saw red. I can't remember the last time I was that angry."

Lull grinned over her teacup. "Just remind me never to whizz you off. I think you're the first woman to ever take on Elven soldiers."

I laughed. "If I'd known what I was doing, I'd never have done it."

The music started up and the floor again filled with dancers. Within a few minutes it seemed as if the incident had never happened.

For whatever reason, the music did not affect me like it had when I first heard it. I was content to remain in the corner and watch the Fae dance. Lull partnered with a man only slightly taller than she and just as round. Short or tall, fat or thin, beautiful or homely, they all shared a love of the dance, and it showed in their happy faces.

Chapter 11
The Huntress

As the last notes of a melody faded to a close, the Bell Tower rang an announcement. Everyone turned to face the musicians.

As I drained my teacup, I felt a presence behind me. I turned my head to see Gid standing there. "It is time for you to come with me," he said, stepping to my side.

"Why?" I asked, still sitting.

"You will find out very shortly." He grabbed my arm and pulled.

"Stop that! You're hurting me!" I cried in alarm.

He ignored my distress and pulled me up from the chair. Then he pushed me ahead of him to a nearby door. Once through, he led me up a flight of stairs, which ended at another door. Opening it with one hand, Gid guided me through with the other. We were standing on the stage, looking out over the ballroom.

"What's going on?" I asked. "Why am I here?"

Gil smiled. "You are about to receive a high honor."

A female Elf wearing a green velvet dress took the stage in front of us. She smiled at the crowd as the musicians started up and began to sing:

Lock your windows and barricade your doors,
Pull closed your curtains and shades.
Extinguish all lights and hide from her sight,
WintersFeast is ebbing; the Huntress rides tonight.

Bloodless wraiths, they will come from the sky,
Pray that you never meet the Wild Hunt's eye.
Riding red-eyed nightmares and wolves at their heels,
The undead Huntress seeks a Human soul to steal.
Walls tumble before them; trees are ripped from the ground,
Death and destruction and Hell-Wolves abound.

The Human will be stood outside on this night,
An offering to appease; Diana's delight.
Chase her, Huntress, and make her your bride,
Follow this Human on an immortal ride.
With free will we give her; take the blood of the Round Ears,
With this sacrifice may you spare us for the next hundred years.

Jasper Reeve came through the doorway and stepped out to the edge of the stage. "GentleFolk, I am pleased to inform you that you are about to witness something stupendous tonight. As you all know, the Wild Hunt of Humans has been a tradition of WintersFeast since the beginning of Fairy history.

"For the first time in three hundred years, we have not been forced to hold a lottery to choose Folk prey for The Huntress. Tonight we have a Human here with us, and she will, as tradition requires, serve as prey."

"In a few minutes the bell will strike twelve. The last stroke of the bell will signal the start of the Wild Hunt and the arrival of The Huntress!"

The audience cheered, whooped, and whistled. My mind raced as I stood on the sideline with Gid still holding my arm in a vice-like grip that hurt. I was to be prey for a Fae Huntress? Could this really be happening?

"Gid, just tell me what's going on!"

"Gid will not tell you, but I will," he said. His features melted and before my horrified eyes, Gid became Adram, who had tricked me before with his shape-changing. I tried to pull away but

116

his grip was just as strong as Gid's had been, despite his now slim physique. His white face and gray-ashed eyes made him look like Death.

The room started to spin and I sagged. Adram shook me. "None of that!" he snapped. "The night is still young. You haven't begun to experience fear yet!"

I remembered to breathe and my head cleared. "What do you want?"

"It is not what I want, but what all the Folk want. We want the Wild Hunt, and tonight we get what we want."

"You intend for me to be chased and killed by a huntress?"

"Not just any huntress. The Huntress and her Huntsmen. The Goddess of WintersFeast, no less. Hunts must have prey. That would be you, Round-Ears!"

He dragged me to the front of the stage and addressed the waiting spectators. "Denizens of Faerie, I present to you the object of the Hunt – the Human!"

He pushed me in front of him so I was looking down at them while the crowd roared approval. As they quieted, I could hear a woman screaming, "No, No!" I recognized the voice – Lull. Two of the Elven soldiers were dragging her toward the main doors.

"Don't do this! She doesn't deserve this! You promised me this wouldn't happen!" Lull broke down into helpless sobs and the soldiers succeeded in removing her from the room.

As I watched, my terror mutated into numbness. I was in mortal danger, yet nothing seemed real. *It isn't really me that they are planning to hunt. It can't be. Gildan wouldn't allow such a thing! But Gildan isn't here, is he? Has he been delayed on purpose? Or is guilt keeping him away?* My mind swirled with questions while my body remained stupefied.

"Hear me, Human. These are the rules of the Hunt. When the bell strikes twelve, the Huntress will arrive. You will be allowed a ten-mile head start. Whenever the Huntress is within one mile of you, she will sound her horn. If you can survive three nights of the Hunt without being killed by the Huntress or her Hunters, you will be allowed to return home to Earth." Adram chuckled. "Of course, if you do survive, you will be the first Human to do so."

My ears heard the words but my brain did not process them. The bell began to toll and my body finally began to respond. I started to shake and I searched the crowd for help. I saw none. The bell sounded the twelfth tone and there were a few moments of utter silence.

A wind howled around the peaks of the building, growing louder and stronger, until the immense crystal chandelier began to sway. Those beneath it moved away nervously.

Mortar dust and bits of stone began raining down on the platform where we stood as well as the ballroom below. Jasper Reeve burst through the door to the stage. "Get out of here now! The Glamour is failing and the building is weak! Run!"

There were sounds of alarm now as the Fae began pushing toward the doors. Blocks of stone followed the dust and mortar, crushing those unfortunate enough to be in their path. Now there were screams as the panicked Fae fought to escape the crumbling building.

Adram finally reacted, though he'd seemed shocked into immobility at first. He shoved me toward the door leading to the staircase. We dodged falling bits of ceiling as we followed the musicians down the stairs. Instead of joining the mob in the ballroom, Adram pulled me to a door at the back of the building.

He reached for the latch and the door was ripped from his hand by the wind. It slammed against the outside wall and revealed a hellish scene. Straw, wood, stone, canvas, market merchandise, and other debris were all caught in the maelstrom, making it dangerous to step outside of the building.

I stared dully at the sight, wondering why I wasn't afraid, and then realized that I was in shock. I'd gone from dancing at a feast to becoming prey in the Wild Hunt in just a matter of minutes.

As suddenly as it had begun, the wind just stopped. Debris fell like a solid rain. An unnatural silence followed. Even the Fae trapped in the ballroom were no longer screaming.

Adram pushed me out the door and we walked around the building to the front. The sight was devastating. The market was gone – only debris and clutter remained. The Grand Ballroom was damaged but still standing. The ceiling had caved in and chunks of stone were missing where it had been slammed by wind-driven objects.

Fae were streaming out the doors, some dragging the injured. Others had stopped and were pointing at the sky. I turned to look, dreading another windstorm, but then saw something much worse. At a distance, but quickly growing larger, I saw glowing men on horseback galloping across the sky toward us. They were accompanied by spectral wolves. The rider in front wore a cloak that streamed out behind her, and her crescent moon horns were silhouetted against the clouds.

The Huntress and her Huntsmen touched ground and trotted toward us. The uninjured Fae fell prostrate before them as they approached. They stopped a few yards from me and Adram. Red-eyed black Hell-Wolves snarled and snapped as the lead rider swung down from her horse.

She was at least six feet tall. Her black cloak shielded her body, and her face was shrouded by a hood; only her yellow eyes shone out of the darkness. She held a spiral horn that looked as though it had come from an animal.

"Goddess of the Hunt, we give you this Human and pray that you are pleased," Adram said.

The Huntress raised the horn to her lips and blew a long, mournful note. Then she pointed at me.

My numbness was pierced by terror and I almost fainted on the spot. Before I could move, Adram pushed me. "Run, you stupid crupper! She will give you only ten miles before she pursues. Go!"

Terrified, I ran. I glanced back to see the Huntress still pointing at me, and my fear intensified, swelling into something almost overwhelming. The wolves wove themselves sinuously around her boots, looking up at her as though for permission to give chase.

Chapter 12
Quentin the Rotter

I ran down the main street and out of the town square into the field where the wagons were parked. I was so hoping that Lull would be there, ready to help me escape, but my hopes were dashed when I saw her empty wagon. Breathing hard, I untied the horses and climbed onto the wagon seat. Zebedee and Nur snorted and pawed the ground, but responded immediately to my awkward signal with the reins.

I managed to get them turned around and onto the road back to Lull's cabin. As much as I wanted them to run as fast as they could, I kept them at a trot. It was much too dark to force the horses to gallop over the rough ground. I bumped along, sure that every hole or bump in the road would be the one to break a wagon wheel.

Oh, God. Oh, God. Ten miles. I have ten miles. Oh, God. Then she blows the horn when she gets close. How long does it take her to travel? Oh, God. Are they on the ground or in the air? It could take seconds. Oh, God. Maybe Gildan will be at the cottage when I get there. Maybe he can get me back home before the Huntress comes.

I grabbed onto that slim hope. *Yes, yes, surely he was just late and is waiting at the cottage to see how WintersFeast went. Oh, God, please let him be there!*

My heart was pounding in my ears and I was gasping for breath. I wasn't cold, but tremors shook my body. Zebedee and Nur seemed to sense my distress, clanking their bits and snorting.

Calm down, dammit! I scolded myself. *I have to think smart. I can't stay at the cottage, that's the first place they'll look. I need supplies. I need to find help. I need food, clothes, water. It's only three days and nights. I can do this. Oh, God!*

Finally, finally, we reached the cottage. It was dark inside but I hopped down from the wagon and ran inside. "Gildan!" I called, then moaned. "Please be here."

There was no answer. The cottage was dark and silent. I wanted to fall to the floor and scream. Instead, I took a deep breath and forced myself to think. I found an empty burlap bag and ran from room to room, gathering supplies. I considered changing into my jeans, shirt, socks and tennis shoes, but then decided not to waste the time. It was time to go.

"I'm so scared," I said forlornly to the empty room. Not giving myself time to think about that, I pulled the cord tight around the neck of my bag and raced back out to the wagon.

I drove the wagon away from the cottage toward the meadows that led to the forest at the base of the mountains. The forest would provide the cover I needed in order to hide. If I could just hide for three nights, it would all be over. Or maybe someone could help me find Gildan, since he had traveled to the mountains to get to Bacchus Yard.

My nerves got the better of me, and I hurried the horses despite the terrain. As we left Agrarian Lea, we passed fewer houses and the road became rougher and hillier. It was as we were coming down one of the hills that it happened.

Out of nowhere, a small shape, blacker than the darkness surrounding us, swooped out of the sky and in a circle around the horses' heads. They reared in fright, neighing their fear. I tugged on the reins, yelling, "Whoa, whoa," but then two more of the shapes dove at my face. I ducked, flinging my hands up to protect my face just as the horses took off.

I fell off the seat and almost off the side of the wagon. Only a last-second grip on the wooden seat saved me. I tried to climb back up onto the seat, but the wagon bounced and thumped over the uneven ground, making it too dangerous. I stayed where I was, yanking on the reins. "Zebedee! Stop! Nur! Stop! Whoa!"

One of the flying creatures came at my face again, and I batted at it frantically. It was close enough for me to see that it was some kind of bat with a humanoid face. The thing leered and chattered as it brushed my hands with its leathery wings.

I screamed, still pulling on the reins. The left front wagon wheel dipped down into a large hole and the wagon jolted, the back end lifting into the air. It came down hard, and the axle broke. A back wheel fell off and the wagon tilted, tilted, and then went over on its side, spilling me onto the hard ground.

When I came to, I was lying partly on the road and partly in the brush. It was still dark, and still cold, and for a moment I was disoriented, unable to remember where I was. With careful movements, I sat up and checked for injuries. My dress was torn and there were painful scrapes on my legs and right arm.

I stood up and looked around but the horses were gone. Fortunately, so were the bat-things. I spent a frantic, fearful few minutes searching for my bag of supplies, and was tremendously relieved to find it a few yards away.

With no other options, I walked down the road toward the forest. Unfamiliar night noises suddenly sounded very loud now that I was alone and there was no wagon noise. The noises also sounded close. Animals. There would be animals in the forest. I stopped and withdrew one of Lull's precious Dirk knives from the bag. I drew the hood of my cloak tightly around my face and trudged on. Surely I was close enough to the forest to be there soon.

Dawn was the most welcome sight of my life. I had been stumbling over exposed roots and had fought my way through brush from the moment I had entered the forest. Unexpected branches had clawed bloody stripes across my face.

I was exhausted, yet too afraid of hearing the Huntress' horn to risk stopping. I had to have traveled over ten miles – surely the Huntress was already on my trail by now.

I couldn't decide whether hearing the horn would be worse than the constant dread of hearing it. Then I remembered that the Hunt was a nightly ordeal. I would have the daylight hours to travel.

I clasped my bag to my chest and kept going. So far, I'd been too frightened and overdosed on adrenalin to feel the cold. But now the new light of day was accompanied by the coldest part of the day, and I was starting to feel it in my hands, nose, and toes.

As I trudged through the woods, slapping branches away with my one free arm, I heard a strange sound – a kind of superimposed grunt and clicking sound. I slowed my pace and gripped my knife tightly, looking all around for the source of the noise.

There was movement in the underbrush about 20 feet to my right. I stopped and stood still, hoping that whatever was emerging wouldn't notice me. A large brown shape with long, wiry fur waddled out of the bushes. A bear!

I wanted to run but remembered that to do so would encourage a chase. It took everything I had to stand there motionless. The bear trundled a few steps closer and then sniffed the air and turned toward me. It growled and I almost screamed. Black pincers, like those of a stag beetle, protruded from the sides of its mouth and were the source of the clicking sounds I had heard.

I could barely breathe; my body felt weak and light. It was all I could do to keep my grip on the knife. I stared at the bear, willing it to go away.

Instead, the bear reared up on its hind legs, towering over me, and roared, clicking its pincers. I screamed and held out the knife as though the bear would know what it was and fear it.

Whap! An arrow shaft pierced the bear between its eyes. It paused in mid-roar and then fell heavily to the ground, dead.

I whirled, searching for the archer. I looked at the sky, expecting to see the ghostly Hunters despite the daylight, but there was nothing among the treetops. I peered into the trees, looking for the flash of elves moving among them, but saw only forest.

The woods around me had fallen silent. I whirled, still holding the knife out in front of me, panting with fear. I had unknowingly been holding my breath and now my body was trying to regulate itself.

The forest returned to life. Insects buzzed and birds claimed territory with song. Wind rustled leaves. Nothing revealed itself.

There was nothing else to do but keep moving, so I forced myself to take that first step, half-expecting an arrow to embed itself in my body. Nothing happened. I kept moving, still gripping the knife so tightly that my hand was losing feeling.

Gradually, my fear lessened as I made my way through the forest. I spent most of the time trying to figure out who the archer was and why he had not attacked me. Had he been a friendly figure, he would have revealed himself. Why help me and then hide from me?

After walking for at least an hour I heard the sound of running water. Following the sound, I discovered a small stream. The streambed was covered with rocks and pebbles that made tiny waterfalls that sparkled in the light of the morning sun.

I was so thirsty! I knelt on the bank and scooped the fresh, clear water into my mouth greedily. It was cold, so cold, but felt wonderful at the same time. Once I was finished drinking, I topped off my waterskin.

As I was returning the skin to my bag, I heard a noise behind me – a rustling, whispery sound. Footsteps, but not quite. I couldn't see anything past the trees but more trees.

It wasn't another bear but there was surely someone or something coming toward me. *It's someone spying on me.* I bet the Huntress has sent a scout! That must be who shot the bear!

I looked carefully but saw nothing more than the forest – evergreens, bare oaks, willows, and maples. The morning sun sent slanted rays down from the treetops, making the forest seem much more friendly than it had seemed in the dark, especially with the night noises.

I relaxed. There was nothing there but a possible bird or squirrel – did Faerie even have squirrels? – so there was nothing to be worried about. My nerves were just frazzled and overreacting to the least little stimulus. Wanting nothing more than to sink down onto the forest floor and rest, I forced my legs to keep moving.

Crack … swish … crack … swish.

Dammit, what IS that? I looked around. There was no movement except for a willow tree's swinging branches. I relaxed again – obviously a bird had just taken flight from the tree. I could hear them greeting the dawn just as they did back home, but I couldn't see them.

Crack … swish … crack … swish.

This time I ignored the noise and kept walking, just a little bit faster.

Crack … swish … crack … swish.

I glanced behind me. Hadn't that willow tree been farther away just a moment ago? I narrowed my gaze to look past it, but the tree close to me was the only willow in the area.

"When I catch you I'm going to switch your legs bloody," muttered a rasping voice.

"What? Hello?" I looked wildly around but I was still alone.

"I'm going to strangle you until your eyeballs pop." Crack … swish.

Oh my God, that tree is walking! And talking! I stared, unable to believe what my eyes and ears were telling me. A narrow, angular, mean face was peering out of the trunk and branches were reaching toward me like claws. Its eyes waggled in crazy circles as the willow lifted half of its roots and stepped toward me … crack … and its branches rustled with the movement … swish.

"I'll poke out your eyes and pull your hair out by the roots," the growly voice promised. The tree lurched forward.

Exhaustion forgotten, I decided not to wait around to find out whether the willow was capable of carrying out its threats. Even I could outrun a tree.

I don't know how long I ran. Sometime later, I came to a small clearing. The sun was up, shining through the branches, and there was soft ground underfoot, covered with pine needles and grass rather than gnarly roots, coarse vines, and prickly bushes. I dropped my bag and sank down into a pool of sunlight. It was warmer now that the sun had risen higher in the sky. I pushed back my hood and lifted my face to the light.

I decided that this was an opportune time to grab a bite to eat before pushing on. The few gulps of water from the waterskin tasted especially sweet to my parched throat. I ate a chunk of bread and decided to hold off on the salty meat until I was sure of more water.

The clearing was a little slice of heaven after forcing my way through the woods. As I ate, I realized that something just didn't feel quite right. After a moment's thought, I realized what was bothering me – the silence. There was no birdsong, no insect chatter, and no small animals rustling around in the brush. There was nothing but a pressing silence.

My feet were aching, so I changed into my socks and tennis shoes. It was amazing how much different it felt to have my own shoes on again. I had been afraid to stop long enough to put them on earlier, but now wished I had.

"Hello, traveler," a scratchy male voice said from the brush at the edge of the clearing.

I whipped my head around, searching for another homicidal willow tree. I grabbed the knife up from the ground where I'd set it when I sat down.

"Oh, dash – don't be afraid," the man said in a concerned tone. "I won't – wouldn't hurt you."

Holding the knife in front of me in what I hoped was a threatening manner, I demanded, "Who are you? What do you want?"

"Quentin. I'm Quentin and I – I just want to – to talk to you."

"Where are you?"

"Over here." He shook a bush, but I still couldn't see him.

"Come out where I can see you."

"Oh – oh, no. I can't," he said. "If I do, you'll have a conniption fit like everyone else."

I brandished the knife to be sure he saw it. This didn't sound good. "Why?"

"Because I'm …" his voice broke. "I'm ugly."

I didn't know what to say to that. As I floundered for a reply, he explained.

"I'm sick and I'm ugly. That's why I'm an outcast. I thought I could at least make friends with the animals, but they run from me, too. All I want is to talk to somebody. It's been such a long time since I've talked to anybody."

His voice was so full of heartache that I found myself believing him. I did wish I could see him, though, so I'd know for sure that he was telling me the truth. Anyone or anything could be hiding in that thick underbrush.

"How long have you been here, Quentin?"

"It seems like forever. I came out here to live as soon as I got sick."

"What kind of sickness do you have? Can other Fae get it? Is that why you're out here alone?"

"It's more of a curse than a sickness, so nobody else can get it. Besides, I'm not Fae, I'm Human."

"Human?" I clutched the knife. "That's impossible! I'm the only Human in Faerie!"

He chuckled, making it somehow sarcastic. "Is that what they told you? Well, I'm Human all right – not that you can tell by lookin' anymore."

I'd had enough of hide-and-seek. "Come out of there and let me see for myself." I glared at the spot where he hid. "Let me see that you're really Human!"

There was a pause. Then his hesitant voice crept past the bushy barrier. "Will you promise not to run away? Please, please don't run away."

"I won't run away." I said, hoping I wasn't lying to him. *Just how horrible does he look? He certainly does sound pitiful.*

The bushes parted and a tall figure stepped into the clearing, blinking rapidly in the winter sunlight. He was definitely sick and he was definitely ugly. His gaunt form was swallowed up by his rough leather clothing. Blue eyes peered from a disfigured face covered with weeping sores. His skin was blackening, rotting flesh.

As if the sight weren't bad enough, the breeze carried the stink of his decomposition into the clearing and I gagged involuntarily. I tried to cover my reaction with a bout of coughing, but he wasn't fooled.

"Now you know why everything alive avoids me." He looked at the ground, then back at me.

"Is it leprosy?" I asked, using strength of will alone to keep me from bolting.

"It's a curse. I don't even know if it has a name. All I know is it's not contagious or anything." Quentin sat heavily on the ground as though he were being pressed down by a huge weight. "It's all right," he said in a voice full of tears. "You can run away now. You've lasted the longest of any so far."

Part of me wanted to accept his dismissal and get as far away from the smell as possible. I should have been disgusted by his appearance, but I could look away from that – the smell was impossible to ignore. Yet I couldn't bring myself to hurt such an already broken man by fleeing from him like he said everyone else had. As awful as this was to witness, it had to be hundreds of times worse to live with it.

"I can stay for a few more minutes, but I can't stay long. I'm trying to find BacchusYard. Do you know if I'm traveling the right way?"

Quentin nodded. "Yes, you're goin' the right way. It's a long way to BacchusYard, though. At least twenty more miles, most of it in the mountains." He paused, then added, "You must be very tired after travelin' on foot all night. You could rest at my diggin's if you wish, before you head out again."

I started to reply, then realized the meaning of his words. "How do you know I've been walking all night?" I asked suspiciously.

He ducked his head. "I saw you," he answered in a low voice.

"You've been following me? For how long?"

He met my eyes with his pain-filled blue ones. "Since before the start of The Wild Hunt."

I stared at him stupidly.

"I always watch WintersFeast," he explained quickly. "I usually manage to sneak a few treats. People leave a lot of good food and drink layin' around unfinished." He smacked his lips. "I really like the drink."

"So you know I'm being hunted," I stated, testing my understanding.

He nodded. "Yes, I know. And I can help you if you'll let me. I've already helped you with the bugbear."

"You! You shot the b—bugbear?"

"I've still got enough fingers and eyesight to use a bow."

He met my eyes for the first time. "I've been involved with the Wild Hunt since I got here," he said in a cold voice, his blue eyes showing the first glints of anger. "I know for a fact that the Huntress can track only at night. I know that if any of the Fae help you they'll become prey, too. There's nobody else in Faerie who can help you but me. They forgot about me."

"How do you know all of this?" I asked, part of me still wary.

"Cause I've been in your shoes. I was hunted." His voice was still cold and angry.

"But I was told that no Human has survived so far!" I objected.

Quentin kept his gaze steady on me. "They lied." He heaved himself to his feet. "I tell you what. Come with me to my diggin's. You can eat and rest and I'll tell you my story."

He saw me stiffen. "I mean you no harm. I have herbs there to counter the smell. Even I can't stand myself sometimes. Besides, I'm in no shape to chase after you if you run."

I was tempted. He did seem to be Human and maybe he could help. Was going with this stranger worth the risk?

He shrugged. "Look around you, woman. Who else is here that you can trust but me? I'm offerin' food, rest, and water." Then he added the *coup de grâce*. "And I can help you survive this thing."

I sat where I was, my mind racing with conflicting thoughts. *Can this sick, smelly man really be who he says he is? Can he really have survived a Hunt? Can he help me find Gildan or win the contest myself? Or is he a trick, a trap set by the Huntress? I can sit here and wait for the Huntress, I can travel on alone and hope for the best, or I can go with Quentin and bolt at the first sign of danger.*

He grunted at my lack of response and turned to walk back into the forest.

My body made the decision before my mind did; I leaped to my feet. "Wait! Quentin, wait! I'm coming with you."

I followed at a distance as he led me through the forest. Soon we stepped onto a path that led to a log cabin built in another natural clearing. The cabin looked as though it had been constructed with giant Lincoln Logs. Trees had been notched and set so firmly in place that no cracks of light showed between them. The roof was wood shingled, and a small covered porch bordered the front of the building. The windows were covered with colorful fabric curtains.

Quentin opened the door, then gestured for me to wait. As he lifted one hand, I saw so many sores covering it that it hurt just to look at it. He left the door open and disappeared inside.

As I waited on the porch, I saw him opening the curtains to let in air and light. He propped open the back door to encourage a cross-current. Finally, he rummaged in a closet or pantry and emerged with bundles of dried herbs. He set them out on the windowsills and at other points in the cabin's front room and then lit them. They began to smolder, thin plumes of smoke rising into the air.

At last he signaled that I could enter. I felt a little bit better about him. What man would go to so much trouble to make the room presentable, just to kill me? I stepped over the threshold and found there was no rotten flesh smell, only a gingery, spicy incense fragrance.

Quentin busied himself starting a fire in the stone hearth. The cabin was much neater than I expected for a sick man living alone. The floor needed sweeping but there was no clutter. A bow and a quiver of arrows hung over the fireplace. A pair of snowshoes and a heavy winter coat hung on pegs on the wall, along with various traps and nets. The furniture, a table and two chairs, were made with the simple, clean lines that hinted at craftsmanship.

"Sit." He gestured toward the table and chairs. "I'll warm up some food while we talk."

His movements were quick and looser than before. He seemed so happy to have my company that I was glad to have made the decision to visit. I was probably his first and only visitor. There was nothing in the cabin that I could see that didn't relate to simple survival. His life seemed devoid of everything but solitude and illness.

Quentin settled a pot over the fire and then came to sit at the table across from me.

"I know you're afraid and don't know who to trust. I know it doesn't mean much right now, but I promise you I only want to help you." He grinned crookedly. "It's the least I can do to repay the lady with no name who has the courage to tolerate me."

I smiled. "I'm Odessa Chase."

"Quentin Collingswood the Third at your service. I'd shake hands, but I can't afford to lose a finger," he said solemnly, then burst into laughter at the appalled expression on my face. "Well, Odessa, which question do you want to ask first?" he asked, once he had stopped laughing.

"I have so many, I don't know which one to pick first," I admitted. "Okay, you say I'm safe during the day?"

"No, not safe, exactly. The Huntress can become corporeal only at night, but she has many eyes and ears during the daylight hours. You must gain as much distance as you can during the day, and don't trust any that you meet along the way." He stood up. "Except for me, of course."

"But how did you survive, Quentin? How did you beat the Huntress?"

He stirred the pot with a long-handled wooden spoon. "Well, when I was brought here in 1897, the Fae didn't realize I was a hunter myself. Back home I spent most of my time in the wilderness, trappin' and sellin' furs till that ran out. Then I hunted for a livin'. That's why it was easy for them to take me. I was alone in the middle of nowhere when I was grabbed."

He returned to the chair across from me. "I don't recall much about it except for a crazy 'dream' about a little green man that piss – uh, sprayed me in the face. Then I woke up in Faerie."

"You were Dusted by a Pixie," I said, and he nodded.

"I know that now. Back then, things was just a blur. I'd only been here a couple of days before I found myself the guest of honor in the Wild Hunt. They never asked about my survival skills and I never told 'em." He chuckled. "You shoulda seen their faces when I began shootin' 'em full of arrows. I think I was the first Human to ever fight back."

"So the Huntress can be hurt? Can she be killed?"

"I don't know about her – never got a clear shot. I was able to keep 'em distracted with trackin' tricks for the first two days. Then, and I think it was just luck really, I was able to fight 'em off with traps and arrows until the dawn of the third day." His voice faded and he sat for a moment, remembering.

"There's one thing you need to know, Odessa. You won't be able to run for three days. You have to bring 'em out of the sky and make 'em touch the ground or anything of it. That makes 'em physical and being physical makes 'em killable." He looked up. "You're gonna have to fight, Odessa."

"I don't have any weapons. I can't shoot like you. How can I fight?"

"I can help you with that but let's eat first." He pushed away from the table and went to the cupboard.

133

"I'll pump some water so you can wash your dishes before you eat," he said, not looking at me. "The stew's boilin', so it's safe for you to eat. I'm not catchin', but there's nothin' wrong with bein' clean. I'll allow you to help yourself."

I got up and washed my dish and fork and filled the bowl with stew without asking any questions. But while I did so, I wondered why his survival of the Wild Hunt was something so hard to talk about that he was now avoiding it.

I ate heartily – the herbs were doing a wonderful job of masking the smell, so my appetite had rebounded with the aroma of cooking food. I drank cup after cup of water since I wasn't sure when the opportunity would come again.

Quentin ate facing away from me. I knew it was a peculiar courtesy on his part and that my watching would have embarrassed him. He was awkward but didn't spill anything or drop his fork.

After we'd eaten, I washed the dishes after a half-hearted protest from Quentin. With my back to him, I finally brought up the subject most on my mind.

"You left off with having fought the Huntress until dawn. Were you told that you could go home if you won, like I was?"

Sitting at the table, Quentin heaved a sigh. It took him so long to respond that at first I thought he was ignoring the question.

"Yes, like you I was promised that I could return home if I won. I was too naïve back then to realize that there's always a price to pay with the Fae, 'specially if you can best 'em. They don't do anything without a plan to ensure they win in the end." He paused and took a long drink.

"I was runnin' out of arrows when the sun began to rise. The Huntress was comin' close to shootin' me – I swear one of her arrows parted my hair. I was firin' down on 'em from the tops of some trees, always firin' and then movin' so they couldn't pin my location. Two of the Hell-Wolves was standin' on their hind legs at the base of the trees, doin' their damnedest to climb. That's when I realized that when they touch the ground they become real – I shot

134

one of the damned things and it died. I went to shoot the other one but my arrows had run out. I thought I was done for but then one little ray of sunshine changed everything."

Finished with the few dishes, I turned around to face him, leaning back against the counter. Quentin was staring off into space as he relived the event.

"I couldn't hear it but the Huntress whistled to the wolves. I only saw her put her fingers to her mouth, but the wolves dropped to the ground and ran to her. Then she pointed at me."

Quentin grimaced. "I hope I never hear that voice again. It was like – like somethin' alive clawin' at my brain. She said, 'You have survived the Wild Hunt. You are free to go back to your home. But will you want to?' Then she laughed, and it was like bugs crawlin' in my ears.

"She got thinner and thinner and more see-through and suddenly was just gone. So was the wolves. I couldn't believe it. I must have sat in that damned tree for an hour, afraid she'd come back soon as I got down. I guess I just couldn't believe I'd actually won.

"Soon as my feet touched the ground, I knew I was goin' home. And I was goin' to change my life when I got back. I was goin' to go see my family, who I hadn't seen in years. Maybe I'd even ask Miss Florence Adkins to marry me. I'd lived through this, and now I was really going to live!"

"I whooped and threw my bow in the air. When I caught it, I noticed a black smudge on my hand. It wouldn't wipe off and it started spreading while I watched. It slithered under my skin like worms. By the time I got back to Agrarian Lea, I looked much as I do now."

"Couldn't any of the healers help you?" I asked. "Isn't there some way to remove the curse?"

Quentin shook his head sadly. "To help me would result in the helper havin' the same fate. Besides, the Huntress is such a powerful evil, I don't think anyone here is her equal. So even though I won the fight, I lost the war. The bitch was right – I could go home, but did I want to? Of course not, not like this! That bitch honeyfuggled me but good!"

"God knows I don't want my family to see me like this. And Miss Florence Adkins, well, I think marriage would be out of the question. Sure, I could go home, but to what? It'd be no different than what I have right here." He gestured at the room. "I had a choice of a prison here or a prison on Earth."

"But modern medicine might be able to help you. It may not cure you, but it could control the symptoms, maybe."

He shrugged. "It's too late now. I'm Human. And I'm over 100 years old. If I was to go to Earth now, my age would kill me before I finished my first breath. I'm stuck here. As long as I stay here, I may not be happy, but at least I'm alive."

I sat down at the table across from him. He had won but the Huntress had cheated him out of his reward. Who was to say the same wouldn't happen to me?

I looked at him sharply. "Quentin, what do you have to gain by helping me?"

"I'm not doin' this for myself," he insisted, leaning forward. "I can help you survive. I can fight with you, fight for you, and help you survive! But I just can't control what the Huntress does afterward."

"But then what?" I demanded. "So either I die during the chase or you help me survive, only to become cursed like you. Those are my only two choices, aren't they?"

"I don't know," he admitted. "Maybe. Probably." He reached out to me with his one almost-good hand and gripped mine. "But if you are cursed, you won't be alone. We can be together."

I wrenched my hand away from him. "So that's it! You want me to survive and be like you. That's what you're counting on, isn't it? You want me to live to be cursed so you won't be alone anymore! Oh my God!"

"Is that so wrong?" He pushed back in his chair and stood, glaring down at me. "I've been alone for at least a century!" he yelled, tears streaming down his ruined face. "So what if that idea came to me while I was watchin' you? What does it matter if I gain a companion from this? Isn't that a better fate than dyin'? Or would you rather die than live with me?"

I didn't answer.

Quentin shoved his chair aside. One of its arms broke off and slid across the wood floor. He stormed out of the cabin without looking back as I shook and wept for him and for myself.

Chapter 13
Gildan and Adram at Odds

Gildan the Silver glared with venomous slitted eyes at Adram, who sat smiling smugly on the unmade bed. "This has gone on long enough."

"Not quite, Good Sir. But soon it will and I will be happy to see the backside of you."

Gildan turned away, clenching his fists and fighting the almost overwhelming urge to strangle the condescending, arrogant pillicock.

"I have been here for over a week. WintersFeast is over. The Hunt has begun. How can I be of any threat to you now?" He struggled to maintain a reasonable tone.

Adram stood up and gestured for the Djinn waiting at the door to take Gildan's plate. "You are right, actually."

Surprised, Gildan turned to face him, then saw the smirk on Adram's face.

"Your little Human has been on the run since midnight last. This is her first full day. You and I both know the Huntress will wait for the third night to come before she kills her."

Adram paused as though thinking. "It would take you a day or more to reach Agrarian Lea from here. By that time she will be on her second day or into her last night. So yes, I suppose I could release you. There is no way you would have time to interfere." Adram opened the door, winked, and said, "But I do not feel generous today." He closed the door and Gildan heard the lock turn.

"Pribbling son of a wazzack," he muttered angrily, starting to pace the small bedroom.

He had tried every trick of verbal war he knew, from anger and threats to docile submission, in order to attain his release. Adram simply laughed in his face or occasionally returned the threats. No one had harmed him, however, and he was being fed. The worst they had done so far was deny him his shoes, and his feet had been cold for days now. All the same, he was being held against his will, and Adram would pay dearly for that.

Gildan was being kept in a cabin at the base of the volcanic Vulcan Mountains directly behind Agrarian Lea. It was Adram's private residence, located near an area of multiple hot springs and boggy marshes called The Steams. The room's window had been boarded over from the outside, but even had Gildan broken through it, there was usually a Djinn guarding it. There was another Djinn on the outside of the bedroom door.

Gildan had never been so angry before in his life. When he got back to Agrarian Lea, his first order of business would be to have Adram replaced. It was bad enough that the Company required a Changeling member at all, but this proved that they were simply too conniving and selfish to serve as objective representatives. Kidnapping a leader of the Company simply to get one's way was beyond unacceptable. The Changelings may not agree, but Poseida and Tempestra would side with him, he was sure.

Gildan sat heavily on the bed, face in hands. There was no way for Odessa to survive The Hunt unscathed. Only one Human had ever managed to thwart The Huntress, and though he lived, his life was a slow death. The Human had possessed woodsman skills that had turned the tables. Odessa, on the other hand, was the oldest and least physically fit of the previous Humans who had been hunted. Too, most of them had lived in Faerie long enough to be at least slightly familiar with the various terrains. No, there was too much working against Odessa for her to come out of this alive.

It's my fault. I never should have brought her here. Gildan's guilt made him cringe. Worst of all, he simply liked her. There was something about the way she listened when he spoke that caused him to enjoy her company. She had a flexibility of mind that allowed her to more easily accept the wonders of Faerie. Others before her had gone insane rather than face the "impossible." He respected her quiet courage. She was afraid, very afraid, but she pushed forward past the fear.

Lull had fallen in love with her Human charge, he could tell. He would sometimes pass the cabin and hear them inside talking and giggling as they did some household chore. Poor Lull. She may not recover from this loss. It had been hard enough for her with the others, but this might be one grief too many for Lull's loving and gentle soul.

How easy it had been for the Folk to see nothing beyond Odessa's race. It had taken only seconds to re-ignite an old adversarial relationship that had faded to almost nothing over time. Apparently the hatred had always been there, a cancer waiting to erupt at the first opportunity.

Sometimes Gildan felt as though he were the only one in all of Faerie to see wisdom in a cooperative relationship with Humans. Now it appeared that his infrequent thought was actually a truth. With Odessa gone, his last chance to rescue Faerie would die with her. There was no telling when or even if another Human would ever be born with the ability to see the Folk. Faerie was on a course of certain destruction, following its diseased sister planet to environmental death.

Gildan lay back on the bed and closed his eyes. He was tired of thinking melancholy thoughts, but that seemed to be all he could do while awake. "Perhaps the end of Faerie is for the best," he mumbled. "Who am I to fight the Gods?"

Morning found Gildan in no better mood. He paced the bedroom, inventing and revising what he would next say to

Adram. He stopped in mid-step when he suddenly realized that the cabin was unusually quiet. He could usually hear Adram's boots treading the wooden floors or the movements of the Djinn just outside the door. Even the dry, ashy smell of the Djinn seemed to have gone. There were no scents or sounds of food being prepared.

He went to the door and listened at the crack. There were no footsteps, no subtle movements. The cabin was utterly still. Gildan grasped the door latch and couldn't quite believe his luck when it turned in his hand. He opened the door carefully, expecting a Djinn to appear at any moment. Nothing happened. He took a step into the hallway and looked around. All of the rooms that he could see were empty.

Gildan walked into the main room. The fireplace was down to a few red embers. The wood had not been replaced overnight. He moved quietly to Adram's bedroom. The door was open, the room empty.

He was truly alone in the cabin. Gildan searched the house and found his cloak and shoes. He put them on quickly, listening for sounds of anyone approaching the cabin. The rudimentary search had turned up nothing he could use as a weapon. He opened the front door, again expecting to be confronted by a Djinn or Adram himself, and was relieved when neither one appeared. He hurried across the porch and into the yard.

It took only a few moments to find a sturdy, six-foot branch he could use both to help with the terrain and to use as a weapon if need be. For whatever reason, Adram had abandoned him here at the cabin, either because of something more important, or because he was simply too cruel to have told Gildan he could go. Gildan suspected the latter.

He started down the path away from the cabin, relief warring with wariness. Adram's idea of a good joke would be to let him get far enough away to believe he had escaped, only to have a Djinn re-capture him.

It took a couple of hours for Gildan to reach the Steams. This was a rocky, sparsely wooded area with hundreds of small hot water streams, spouts, and geysers. The sublayers of the ground were so hot that even the rocks and boulders could be hot to the touch. In places steam rose in tendrils into the cooler air above.

Some of the trees and vegetation had adapted to the above-normal temperatures, but others had not. Gray, dead brush and fallen trees littered the terrain. The going was slower here, as Gildan had to test pools before stepping into them or chance a burn.

He was so busy muttering threats toward Adram that he almost didn't see the turtle in time. While navigating a warm stream, one foot slipped on the muddy bottom. His hand flew out to a nearby boulder for balance, nearly hitting a turtle sunning itself on the top of the rock. The red and orange turtle hissed, and Gildan jerked his hand away just in time to avoid a nasty burn from the turtle's fiery breath.

From then on he waded carefully, using his stick to prod pools that may have hidden other dangerous fauna. The brightly colored fish that changed colors according to whim were of no concern and nor were the steam-breathing lizards. There were, however, electric snakes that used a pulse of electricity to stop the heart, and leeches that burned their way into flesh.

Gildan pressed on. He couldn't help hoping Odessa was still alive. Not only did she have to worry about the Huntress, but any Folk she encountered would also be dangerous to her. They could not kill her – that was forbidden – but they could toy with her and delay her escape. If she was still alive, this was the last daylight she would see. The Huntress would close in for the kill once night came again.

If only I could have stopped it. If only I had never brought her over. If only … the "if onlies" are a waste of time. There is nothing I can do to help her now. But there is plenty I can do to make Adram pay for his part in her death.

Tired and ill-tempered, the usually peaceful, stolid, deliberate man who represented the tillers of Faerie impulsively used his staff to knock the next Flame Turtle he saw into the water.

Chapter 14
Swimming With Moose

uentin was on my mind, and when he returned, I knew what I would say to him. I had washed my face and composed myself by tidying up the room. I had righted the broken chair, then found a broom and swept the floor.

"I'm sorry," Quentin said from the threshold. "I didn't mean to frighten you. Or upset you."

"I'm glad you came back before I left," I said. "I didn't want to leave things like this."

He stepped into the room and I motioned him to the chair. He closed the door carefully and took his seat, watching me for clues about how I was feeling.

"I've had some time to think," I began, folding my hands on the table. "I don't like my options, but I do agree with you that I need your help."

He straightened his back and then met my gaze, his blue eyes brightening.

"I do have to tell you that if I do survive this and end up cursed, I'll go home anyway. I have faith that modern medicine can keep it manageable," I faltered, then pushed on. I hated doing this to him. His loneliness wasn't his fault and he wasn't to blame for trying to find a solution for it. "What I need from you is to know whether or not you'll still help me, knowing I don't plan to stay here."

Quentin slumped in the chair. He looked so dejected that I felt guilty for squashing his hopes.

"I know you're not a bad man, Quentin. And I know you're desperate for companionship. But I can't live here like you do. I just can't!"

He stared at the tabletop. "Because I'm so horrible."

"No, your curse isn't the reason I can't stay. I can't stay because I don't belong here."

"And you think I do? Because I'm a monster?" His voice had risen but he still wouldn't look at me.

"You're not a monster, not to me. If you were a monster, you'd have held me for the Huntress instead of giving me food and rest and safety. I know you're a good man. Believe me, I wish I could say that I'd stay here with you, but I can't."

"Remember when you first realized that you had won the Hunt and were planning to go home and change your life? Well, while you were gone, I realized that I have that same choice. I want to go home and change the way I live. I want to be more social, maybe find a husband, and push my career forward rather than just letting things happen."

"It's different for you, Quentin. The world you came from has moved on. But there's a chance that mine is still there. If it is, I want to go. And even if it's not, I want to try. Even if time has passed on Earth so that I die when I go back, I still want to go home."

At that moment there was a loud THUNK! against the cabin's front door. We both jumped at the unexpected sound and looked at the door. Quentin signaled for me to stay where I was. He went to the door on quiet feet and listened before opening it a crack and looking out.

He swung the door open suddenly, prepared to do battle, but there was no response. Instead, an arrow was stuck in the door with a piece of paper on the shaft. I hurried over to look as Quentin pulled the arrow from the door and pulled off the note. It read:

GIVE HER TO US ROTTER OR DIE

Quentin balled the paper in his fist and cursed. I turned and ran to where my bag lay in a corner and grabbed my cloak from its wall peg.

"What are you doing?" Quentin asked as he slammed the door shut.

"I'm leaving! They know I'm here!" I was panicking. My chest was so tight with fear that I had trouble drawing breath. "You can tell them I escaped from you." I took the big knife out of the bag and straightened to find Quentin standing in front of me.

"I'm comin' with you," he stated firmly.

There was a volley of sharp sounds at the front door.

"Elves," Quentin snarled. He ran to the fireplace and grabbed his bow and quiver. "Come on, out the back. I can cover us."

He opened the back door a crack. I expected to hear quills or arrows hit it the instant it moved, but all was still. He opened it wider, looked out, and then took a step outside, arrow nocked in his bowstring. Again there was no reaction.

"It's a trick, but we have no choice. They'll burn down the cabin if we don't leave. If they really wanted to kill us, they'd have surrounded the cabin, not just attacked the front. Follow me." he ordered, walking forward.

We got to the forest edge on the other side of the clearing. An arrow thunked into a tree beside me. It had come from the direction of the cabin. The Elves were moving toward the back of the cabin and at least one had seen us.

"Best we can do is go where they wouldn't expect us to. Go straight through the woods til you see a twin oak. Then go left, to the lake. There'll be a stand of boulders. I'll hold 'em off here and meet you there," Quentin hissed, loosing an arrow. There was a yelp as it met its target.

I fled, trying to run as quietly as I could while still making time. At least it was daylight and I could see all the obstacles in my way rather than blindly stumbling over them like I had in the night.

I was worried about missing the twin oaks among all the other trees in the forest, but it turned out to be a needless worry. They were huge, both trees splitting from a single trunk that was yards around. They were magnificent – obviously hundreds or probably even thousands of years old.

I stopped for a few moments to catch my breath and listen. There were the usual forest sounds of birdsong and buzzing insects. That meant Quentin must still be occupied with the Elves and not close behind me. I hurried on, desperately hoping that I wouldn't encounter an enemy and be forced to use the knife.

I looked at the knife clutched in my hand. It gave me a sense of safety, but was it really? I'd never been forced to use a knife as a weapon before. Part of me wondered if I was capable of using one that way, even in self-defense. I imagined how it would feel to thrust that razor-sharp blade into a living being rather than a dead chicken, and I shuddered.

This knife was so sharp that it probably wouldn't be felt until the damage to organs and arteries had already been done. I had read once that most people who had been stabbed never felt anything more than a perceived punch.

"Stupid," I muttered. *Here I am running for my life, imagining a life-or-death struggle, and I'm worried about whether or not it will hurt my enemy? Wasn't hurting them the whole point?*

If it came down to it, would I wound or kill to save my own life? I tilted the blade and watched it reflect light. *Yes,* I decided, *if I had no other choice, I could use the knife.* After all, if I acted like one of those stupid, screaming women in the movies, I would die of shame. Still, I hoped I would never have to test my theory.

When you're fleeing for your life, time plays tricks on you. On one hand, time seems to slow to a crawl as you anticipate reaching a place of safety. Yet at the same time, it seems to fly when you imagine how close your pursuers must be. I was bone-tired, but thoughts of facing the Elves kept me moving. I'd seen only a little of what the Elves were capable of, and I didn't want to be at their mercy until nightfall when The Huntress would reappear.

The day was bright but a chilly wind forced me to pull up my hood. I didn't like how it interfered with my peripheral vision, but my ears were freezing. I noted the remaining leaves on the trees were turned upside-down by the wind. My grandmother used to say that when you saw the undersides of the leaves, the wind was bringing rain. I hoped this didn't prove true in Faerie as it did at home. It felt almost cold enough for any moisture to fall as snow, but if it didn't freeze and just fell as rain, that would be even more uncomfortable.

I headed left from the monster twin-trees and trudged on, looking back a couple times to admire the huge oaks and marvel at how they'd survived here for such a long time. I tried avoiding overhanging vines and low branches, ankle-twisting surface roots, and slippery pools of pine needles. Needless to say, every sound in the surrounding brush caused me to flinch and point the knife, sure that an Elven soldier would appear.

I was also worried about Quentin. I needed and wanted his help, but I also didn't want to involve him in my struggle. I knew that no matter what he said, or even left unsaid, that he would be secretly hoping that I would end up staying with him.

I didn't really blame him – he wouldn't wish me any harm if my options weren't so limited. To him, being cursed was better than death. I couldn't disagree with that, but I also couldn't ignore the fact that I might be able to recover from the curse.

There had been times in my life when I'd found myself wishing for the comfort of a companion. While I was happy enough with my solitary life most of the time, I could seek out companionship when loneliness came. Quentin could not. I couldn't imagine being totally alone for 100 years without even the company of a pet.

How could I blame him for hoping things would turn out his way? I was probably the only chance he'd ever get of having a companion. Not only would I be sharing his affliction but I would truly understand it, and that kind of appeal can't be denied.

Neither of my two options appealed to me, but of the two, I believed I was making the best choice. I didn't know much about rotting diseases, but I did know that there had been many medical advancements in the treatment of leprosy, which seemed similar to

Quentin's curse. We were long past years-ago "solutions" of confining victims to leper colonies.

I felt bad that I would have to leave Quentin behind, but I just didn't see any other choice. Suddenly inspired, I stopped dead in my tracks. Gildan could travel between worlds! Surely he could deliver any medicines I discovered helpful to Quentin for me. If Quentin could manage the symptoms, he could live a relatively normal life in Faerie, no longer a hermit.

I grinned. This was even more reason to beat The Huntress. I may lose the war, but that didn't mean I had to surrender. Humans could be just as conniving as the Fae. All I had to do was stay alive, and with Quentin's help that didn't seem like such a far-fetched idea.

At last the forest began to thin, and I caught glimpses of water in the distance. Thank God. If I had to go much farther, I'd probably collapse. Every muscle in my body ached. I was too old and fat for all of this!

At the forest's edge I stopped and scouted the lake area. The lake was so wide that I couldn't see the other side, but there seemed to be no unnatural movement in the areas I could see. Of course, there was no way to know who or what might be concealed in the shadows past the perimeter of the trees.

The lakeshore was rocky, and I spotted the stand of boulders where Quentin had said he would meet me. I looked around once more, and then pushed on toward them. I would just have to take the chance that there were no Fae lurking and waiting for me.

The boulders were arranged in a formation that created a cozy space between them. I checked the ground for snakes before dropping my bag and myself. The rocks shielded me from the wind, but I was still cold. There was no sunlight in this space to warm the rock and the air.

I took a few minutes to retrieve my jeans and put them on under my dress. The extra layer did the trick. I sat down and leaned my back against the rock wall. The light was dim and I was finally warming up. My ears were burning, which meant they were thawing. I took a small drink of water and then leaned back with a sigh. Quentin would be here soon.

When I woke up, the shelter was dark. I looked around wildly – had a noise awakened me? It came again, the sound of splashing water. Was it Quentin? I jumped to my feet and peered out of the narrow passage between the boulders.

A moose was knee-deep in the water, drinking. Water dripped from its massive muzzle as it came up to breathe. It had no antlers, so I assumed it was a cow or a large calf. Either it didn't know I was spying on it or it didn't care. It continued to drink.

I crept out of my shelter and looked around for signs that Quentin had arrived while I was asleep. If he had, I was sure he would have checked the interior of the boulders for me.

Gray clouds covered the sky, making judging the time of day difficult. It felt like late afternoon. Unless he had run into serious trouble, he should have been here by now. Surely I had slept at least a few hours. Worried, I checked the ground for footprints, but not really knowing what I was looking for, I had no success.

Now what? Should I continue to wait, or travel on alone? I couldn't afford to waste daylight hours – they were my best bet for putting distance between me and The Huntress. A spike of fear pierced my body – could The Huntress become corporeal in a false darkness like this? Going back to the cabin was out of the question. By the time I made my way there, night would definitely have fallen. Besides, the Elves would have reported the cabin as my last known location.

As much as I hated and feared to go on alone, I knew it was what I should do. I decided to leave Quentin a clue to my direction, maybe in the dirt of my rock shelter. I was making my way back into the boulders when I heard a woman's voice call out.

"Haaalllooo." It was a deep voice, but still female.

I looked up to see a morbidly obese woman coming out of the shallow water of the lake. Her skin was reddish-brown and her dark brown hair was so long it nearly covered her shapeless dress.

Suddenly Fairies

As she approached the shore, I saw she had the largest nose I had ever seen on a humanoid face. Wide, bulbous and slanted downward, it completely dominated her face.

My instant Fae-fear must have shown on my face, for she stopped ankle-deep in the water. "Please don't be afraid. Quentin sent me."

"How do I know that's true?" I asked, side-stepping a little closer to the opening in the boulders.

"He said you would be suspicious of any Fae, but he had no choice but to send me. He said there were Elves following him so he couldn't come to you himself." She stood there trying to appear as harmless as someone her size could. She was tall in spite of her obesity and her arms and legs were too long in proportion to her torso. Under her heavy curtain of hair, large brown eyes regarded me.

I stared at her, saying nothing, trying to decide what to believe. *Can she be telling the truth? Or is this a Fae ploy to trap me?*

"Where is Quentin?" I demanded.

She turned and pointed across the lake. "He's on the other side, waiting for you. He sent me because I can get you across the lake."

"Tell me where he is and I'll go around the lake."

She laughed, a braying sound. "It will take you hours to walk around the lake. I can have you across in minutes. I don't know your whole story, but Quentin said you didn't have a lot of time to waste."

"And how can you get me across?" I looked pointedly at the water around her. "I don't see a boat."

"I don't need a boat. I can carry you."

"I don't think so," I said, "You're big, but I'm no featherweight."

She waded onto the shore and I saw her feet. They were split into two large hooved toes. "I didn't say I would carry you in this form. Quentin knew what he was doing when he asked me to do this. Trust him."

"You're the moose I saw earlier, aren't you?" I'd never heard of a were-moose before, but I supposed anything went in Faerie.

"Yes. I wanted to be sure you were here and I can swim faster as a moose." She gestured at her body. "This form floats too much."

I couldn't bring myself to just go along with her. Maybe I was being paranoid, maybe not. Maybe my fear of being falsely paranoid was complicating a simple situation. Or maybe I should trust the paranoia.

"Look, I have young to feed," the woman said, finally sounding cross. "I can't stand around here all day waiting for you to make up your mind. It's up to you. Either come with me or walk miles around the lake. I'll tell Quentin I tried but you wouldn't trust me – or him."

I looked again at the expanse of lake. What if she was right and Quentin was waiting for me on the other side? How could she have known I was here if Quentin hadn't told her?

The woman turned to go back. "I'll tell Quentin you refused. He'll have to figure out another way to meet you."

"No, wait," I said, "let me get my bag and I'll come with you."

She looked back over her shoulder and smiled. "I'll be right here. Just climb on and hold tight."

Still confused, but hanging onto the idea that action was better than inaction, I walked into the shelter and retrieved my bag. On impulse, I scratched "across lake" into the sandy dirt, just in case I was making a huge mistake and Quentin happened to come looking for me here after all.

I came out of the shelter to find the female moose resting on the shore, legs tucked underneath her body. I tied my bag to my wrist. It was much lighter now that I was wearing my jeans.

It was a bit of a climb to get onto the moose's back. She had a thick, strong neck and a long-haired hump on her shoulders. I leaned across the hump and hugged her neck.

I thought for sure that I would slip backward, right off her back end, when she stood up front legs first. Fortunately, she got her hind legs beneath her and leveled off before I lost my grip. I wasn't much of a horse rider, so it was an impressive feeling to be sitting up so high on such a massive animal. I could feel her muscles working beneath me as she waded into the water.

Her legs were so long that it was quite a distance before she actually had to swim. I drew my legs up to keep from getting wet – it was cold enough without being wet, too. I was practically lying across her back above the surface of the icy water.

We were almost halfway across the lake when I felt the moose's massive body start to change shape. With a yelp, I lost my grip and slid into the cold water. The water closed over my head and I had to fight my heavy cloak, dress, and jeans, all soaked with water and pulling me down. I managed to break the surface and take a gasping breath, but then the obese woman treading water next to me gripped my shoulders and pushed me back under.

I flailed my arms and felt my bag hit me in the face, still tied to my wrist. I twisted away from the woman's bruising grip but she still had my cloak. I couldn't free myself, and I had to breathe! I tore the bag open, fighting the urge to breathe in water. I reached into the bag and grabbed the first handle I felt. I withdrew the knife and blindly plunged it upward.

She shrieked. The water around me turned red. I had to breathe! I forced my way toward the surface and was almost there when the woman grabbed my hair and pushed me down again. I breathed in water.

I felt no fear. It was peaceful, floating beneath the surface. I could see light above me, but it was merely a pretty vision without meaning. The water around me now felt like a warm bath.

The woman floated above me and blocked out part of the light. She was bleeding, and her blood clouded up in the water before dispersing. I watched the patterns. I knew I was dying. I felt a brief flicker of triumph – I was cheating The Huntress out of her kill. Darkness began at my peripheral vision and slowly my sight faded to a depthless black.

Chapter 15
Led Astray

The Huntress fronted her Huntsmen across the leaden sky, her yellow eyes gleaming in the false twilight. Green flames flickered from the eyes of her mount, an enormous black stallion. Sparks flew from its hooves like tiny bolts of lightning.

The Huntsmen's black and grey cloaks matched their steeds, and they whooped war cries as the pack raced the skies. Some were little more than skeletons with bits of flesh still attached to their bones, damned things that could not die. Others were complete spirit – death gods that had fallen out of favor. Hell-Wolves accompanied the horses, their hot breath steaming as they panted and howled. Their red ears matched their flashing eyes.

The Pack reached the lake and the air shivered with the force of The Huntress' rage at the sight of the bloated body floating on the lake and the dark shadow of the smaller form below the surface. Her horse hovered over the water and she slid halfway down to reach into the water. She grasped the limp figure of her prey, wrenched her up from the water, and then flew with her to the shore.

Behind her, two of the Huntsmen carried the moose-woman between them. She struggled briefly and hit the ground with a thump and a moan of pain.

The Pack descended as The Huntress dismounted and faced the lake, standing over the drowned body. The Huntress made a circular gesture. A waterspout formed on the lake's surface and moments later, stopped whirling to reveal Poseida, Lady of the Undines. Her large eyes were wide and terrified as she looked at The Huntress.

The goddess gestured toward Odessa's limp body. "Bring her back," she demanded. "I will not be cheated."

Poseida approached and knelt beside Odessa. The Human was not breathing. Poseida placed a hand on her chest above the water pooled in her lungs. Poseida began to speak in a voice like water boiling in a pot. The water in Odessa's lungs evaporated. In moments, her hair and clothing were dry. But still she did not breathe.

Poseida looked up. "I have done what I can do. I cannot restore life where there is none."

The Huntress roared.

Poseida flinched but stood her ground. "I cannot do anything more."

The moose-woman lay on the ground beside Odessa, the hilt of the knife protruding from her belly. She looked up at the Pack and mewled with fear. "I didn't mean to drown her. I was bringing her to you like you said, and it just happened. I didn't mean to!"

The Huntress made a furious gesture and a Huntsman stepped forward with an arrow nocked in his bow. His skeletal fingers drew back the arrow and released it. It pierced the moose-woman's left eye and broke through the back of her skull, ending her whimpering.

Still in a fury, the Huntress drew back her booted foot and violently kicked Odessa. The force of the blow drove her body onto its side. Poseida caught her before she landed on her face. Odessa coughed.

"She is breathing!" Poseida announced.

Odessa, groggy and confused, rolled back onto her back and saw a beautiful woman's face hovering over hers. The woman's veils were blue and embedded with crystals. The veils flowed from her headdress like a waterfall of silk. Her large blue-green eyes were kind, but seemed frightened.

When Odessa tried to speak, the woman hushed her and placed a gentle hand over her eyes so she wouldn't see The Huntress or the Pack.

"Sleep. You will be all right. Just rest for a few moments," Poseida murmured, glancing up nervously at The Huntress.

The death goddess signaled the Huntsmen to mount. With a sound like thunder, the Hunters followed her across the lake and back into the sky. The Hunt was not over.

Poseida took one last, sad look at Odessa before returning to the lake.

"May your God bless you," she said, and then she melted into the surface of the lake.

It was dark and something was tickling my face. I lifted a hand to bat it away. I was lying on the cold ground and flakes of snow were falling from the darkened gray sky.

As soon as I sat up and saw the lake, my memory flooded back. The moose-woman had betrayed me and had held me under until I drowned! So how had I come to be here on the shore, alive and dry except for melting snowflakes?

I looked to my right and spasmed with shock. The moose-woman lay a few feet away, my knife in her belly and a large arrow shaft through her head. I scrambled away from the corpse. That arrow – it was much too large to be Elven.

"Quentin?" I called out.

There was no response. I didn't want to, but I looked at the arrow again. A crawly feeling in my stomach told me what I didn't want to know. That arrow belonged to The Huntress, who had killed her because she had tried to take the prize. But why had she left me alive?

My heart sank a little as I realized the answer. She hadn't killed me because she wanted the game to go on. She was toying with me, allowing me hope that I would reach the third night and survive it. She wanted the stalk before killing me. There was no thrill with unconscious prey. She wanted me to run until the very end.

I felt hopeless, exhausted, and miserable. Part of me wanted to just give up and let her kill me just to be done with this. This was only the second night of the Hunt. I couldn't imagine running another 36 hours. I cried my misery out as snow collected on my cloak and covered the dead moose-woman's blood.

I was cried out and wiping my eyes when the hazy memory of a veiled woman came to me. Soothing words and a calming touch. Who was she? How did she figure into this? A flicker of hope ignited in my chest. She could tell others, maybe even Quentin. Perhaps she was even now summoning help for me.

I have to stay alive in case someone comes. My bag was still tied to my wrist but felt very light. I opened the loose neck wider and looked inside. All that remained were a couple of candles, the waterskin, and a few strips of dried beef that had been trapped by the skin. My blouse, the second knife, and the fire starter were probably at the bottom of the lake.

My eyes strayed back to the corpse and my knife.

"Oh, God," I whined, "I so don't want to do this."

Keeping my gaze on the snowy ground directly in front of me, I crawled toward the corpse. When I could see the silver hilt of the knife, I gritted my teeth and swallowed against the building nausea, and reached for the knife.

A horn sounded from the other side of the lake. This was no time for squeamishness. I yanked the knife free of the moose-woman's body, scrambled to my feet, grabbed my bag, and ran headlong into the forest.

Panic drove me through the undergrowth and brush for quite a while before I had to slow down. When I did, I saw that this part of the forest was less dense than where I had traveled from

Agrarian Lea. I hoped this meant I was nearing the base of the mountains that would lead me to BacchusYard and Gildan.

The snow that had lightly patted me awake was increasing in volume, coming down steadily now as I strode through the forest. I imagined the Huntress and her awful wolves less than a mile behind me, which made my body try to outrun my mind. My tennis shoes weren't the best things to be wearing in snow and I slipped and slid in places but managed not to fall. I gasped for air, and my knees and ankles hurt with each step, but my fear overshadowed the pain.

The forest finally thinned even more and I thought I saw rocky outcroppings ahead. Strangely, although it was snowing here in the forest, the rocks ahead were dark with moisture rather than white from accumulated snow. As I grew closer, the air warmed, and the snow turned to rain.

Steam rose lazily in the heavy, wet air from pools and small streams interlaced in the distance. Rain made soft pattering sounds on my cape as I made my way out of the trees and onto the open, rock-strewn ground. I picked my way across the pebbly, stony, slippery terrain.

Before I knew what had happened, something slammed into me and I went down hard, cracking my shoulder against a boulder as I fell. The wolf whirled around and closed its jaws over my left foot. It began dragging me back toward the forest as I screamed and clawed the ground for handholds.

There was a high whistling sound and then a thunk of steel meeting bone. An arrow jutted from the top of the wolf's head. Reflexively it bit down harder before releasing my foot and folding to the ground. I yanked my foot away from it, then smelled a familiar stench.

"Quentin!" I scrambled to my feet and yelped as blood flowed from my bitten ankle.

He came out of the trees carrying his bow. I limped toward him as he looked around for enemies.

"Past the Steams are some caves. We can hide there and I can easily defend it." He gestured with the bow for me to go ahead of him.

The wolf's teeth had punctured my skin and maybe grazed bone; it ached but I could still hold my weight.

"Quentin," I asked over my shoulder, "will a Hell-Wolf bite do anything to me? Will I turn into a werewolf or something?"

He snorted a laugh. "No, you will not turn into ..."

His words were drowned by a peal of thunder so close that the vibrations thrummed throughout my body. It was followed by a gust of wind and the yells of the Huntsmen. A wolf howled. In front of us, the Huntress and her followers were descending from the sky.

The Huntress stared at me with her glowing yellow eyes; she had me lined up in her bow's sight even before her monstrous horse touched the ground. There was no place to hide, no place to run. I was almost relieved that the chase was finally over. I tensed, waiting for the piercing pain that was to come.

"Go!" Quentin yelled to me as he stopped and faced the Huntsmen. He released arrows one after the other while yelling for me to run.

Quentin was now a few yards ahead of me, letting arrows fly as fast as he could draw his bow. I saw arrows protruding from some of the Huntsmen who were still flesh, but the Huntress herself was unharmed, just sitting and staring at me, obviously relishing my terror.

I stared back at her, knowing that running was useless. My legs were liquid and trembling, and tears formed in my eyes, but I refused to show her any more weakness. I would not die pleading with a monster.

The Huntress turned suddenly and I heard the chilling sound of steel through flesh. An arrowhead punched through the back of Quentin's neck and I screamed in horror. I ran to him and grabbed his arm.

"Run," he gurgled past the blood in his mouth and throat. His knees buckled and he fell with me still hanging onto his arm.

The Huntress and her band trotted toward me, the lead horse's eyes shooting lightning bolts and its hooves striking sparks on the stony ground. I screamed at them in wordless fury as the horses whirled, moments before they would have trampled us beneath them.

I looked down at Quentin. He was no longer bleeding – or breathing, either. His chest was still and his good eye wide and unblinking. A huge pool of blood surrounded his throat and head. I held his arm and screamed until my voice gave way and only ghosts of my despair drifted to my ears.

I walked mindlessly until dawn, no longer afraid or even angry. I couldn't even cry, I was that numb. I walked through forest and meadows and over rocks. If I fell, I hardly noticed; I just picked myself up and walked on. The rain had stopped at some point after I had reluctantly left Quentin's body, but I had paid no notice to that, either.

I came to an area of hot springs and had to slow my pace to avoid stepping into the simmering pools. Steam rose from some, others gently boiled. I was almost immediately overheated in my heavy dress and jeans but I didn't want to waste time changing out of my jeans.

As I stepped over a small pool, a tiny bright red frog popped to the surface. Before I could finish my step-over, the frog spit a stream of hot water onto my leg. I yelped – I could feel it even through my jeans. Good thing I hadn't removed them after all.

I hopped over the pool and from then on crossed around rather than over as many pools as possible.

A while later, I was still among the hot springs but could see trees and mountains ahead. Then movement caught my eye as a small shape peeped at me from behind a boulder.

"Hello?" I called, changing direction so that I could approach the figure.

The peeper did not answer but it came out of hiding. I saw a female Gnome, only a foot or so tall. Her red pointed cone of a hat topped long braids of dark hair. Her tiny features were perfect and doll-like. Her dress and apron mimicked the colors of the forest.

She gestured "Come here," but I hesitated.

"Can you tell me if I'm close to Bacchus Yard?"

The Gnome only gestured with agitation and turned back the way she had come. Afraid of losing my only possible source of information, I hurried after her.

She walked into the gloom of the surrounding forest and then all I could see was her red hat bobbing ahead of me.

I tried to catch up to her, but no matter how quickly I walked the gnome was always a short distance ahead of me. I stopped in my tracks when it suddenly occurred to me that she may be leading me straight to the Huntress.

"Hello? Where are you taking me?"

The Gnome stopped, turned, and put a finger to her lips as she looked to the sky. I understood the message – be quiet or the Huntress would hear my voice. I realized that her silence was also a precaution since death was the punishment for any Fae who helped the hunted. Apparently she *was* on my side, after all.

The Gnome hurried ahead and I followed. We walked for a long time. I was exhausted, thirsty, and hungry. I could walk for only so long before I had to take a break. Every time I did so, the Gnome made her displeasure known by stamping her tiny feet and motioning for me to follow her.

After traveling in this fitful manner for what seemed like hours, the trees thinned out. I saw a meadow dotted with long grasses that danced in the wind.

Once we had traveled halfway across the meadow I saw a sight that filled me with joy. I forgot all about my pain and exhaustion. Ahead was a tall stone fence with a wrought-iron gate. A sign above the gate announced "BacchusYard."

I was so excited that for the first time I overtook the Gnome, almost stepping on her in my rush to reach the gate. I lifted the latch holding the gate closed and stepped through – and fell into space.

There was no gate, no BacchusYard. I had walked off of an embankment. I hit the steep side of the hill and rolled down, coming to a stop only when I landed in shallow river water. The shock of the cold water made me flail and sputter and I jumped up, wet, betrayed, and furious. Other than a few bruises from falling on rocks and brush, I was unhurt – except for my pride.

The Gnome appeared at the top of the embankment and exploded into shrill laughter. She morphed out of the Gnome figure and into a Goblin. Now about three feet tall, with a misshapen head, long, stringy hair, bulging eyes, and a bony crooked body, the goblin clapped its contorted hands and danced with glee.

The high-pitched laughter plucked my last nerve. After all I had been through, the cruelty of the BacchusYard illusion was just too much to bear. I hiked up my sodden dress and climbed onto the riverbank. Then, still enraged, I clawed my way up the side of the embankment.

The Goblin was too busy celebrating to notice until I pulled myself up onto the ledge. He stopped in mid-dance and goggled at me. I must have looked a fright, even to a Goblin, with my dripping clothes and hair and a furious grimace on my face.

He turned to run.

"Oh no you don't, you little bastard!"

I ran up behind him and gave him a very satisfying foot to the ass. He went airborne with a surprised "oof," followed by a thump as he hit the ground.

I raced to the prone figure and raised my foot to stomp him. Stunned, he looked up at me and his eyes bugged out even more with terror. He squeaked.

I hesitated, then lowered my foot.

"Get out of here before I change my mind," I snarled. "Go while you still can."

The Goblin rolled over and stood up. He walked a short distance away, then turned. "Round-ears!" he hooted, gave a giggle, and then was quickly lost in the tall grasses of the meadow.

I was too tired to care about his final insult. It was then that I realized that the Gnome and I had been walking far longer than it had seemed. The sun was low, almost behind the trees. It would be twilight in a matter of minutes rather than hours.

The Huntress had sent the Gnome to waste away the day so that I could not gain distance during the daylight hours when she was powerless. The urge to give up and let her end this hellish experience overpowered me. I sank to the ground, exhausted. *Quentin's gone, I'm alone, there's no hope left. I give up. I can't do this anymore!*

I looked at the low-hanging sun already casting shadows over the land. Wait! If the Huntress was desperate enough to make me waste a day, that must mean I'm close to BacchusYard! Otherwise she wouldn't have needed to stop me!

I stood up, wiped my face, smoothed my hair, and started walking across the meadow back to the hot springs. I had glimpsed mountains just beyond the springs and I knew that the real BacchusYard was somewhere on the other side of them.

Finally, the dark outlines of stone formations rose into the sky ahead. It was a relief to walk on a smooth surface again after the squishy earth and slippery rocks of the springs. Quentin had said there were caves in this area, and I hoped to find one amongst the peaks ahead.

I noticed that the left side of my neck was stiff. I must have hurt it when I fell. I flexed it and gave my shoulder and neck a rub. Then I looked up at the mounds of rocks ahead and stopped short, my eyes widening. The face of the cliff was nearly vertical, but above the cliff wall I could see shadows of what could be the mouths of caves.

Full of dread, I forced myself forward. I had to find shelter fast. I couldn't think about being fat and clumsy; climbing was my only choice. Unless I found a hiding place I would be an easy target for The Huntress. It would be hard, even for her, to find me in a dark cave at night.

At first it was fairly easy to walk up the slope at the foot of the cliff, though the terrain was rocky and I had to weave my way through fallen boulders. The hill slanted upward and peaked about one-fourth of the way up the cliffside. A few pine trees were scattered across the hillside, offering me a bit of screening as I made my way up.

I stopped at the top of the hill and studied the cliffside before me, looking for places that would allow me the best hand- and footholds. I kept thinking I just wanted to quit – this was going to be too hard! I'd never climbed anything higher than a ladder to change a light bulb – what if I fell? What if I got stuck?

Then the wind picked up, bringing with it the sound of distant thunder – the Huntress! I hurried off the hill and to the cliff face, shaking from fear, stepped onto a tiny ledge, and began to work my way up. It was hard, hard work, most definitely the hardest thing I'd ever done. I moved upward inch by inch. It seemed to take forever.

My foot kicked some small stones and I heard them tumble and bounce down the side of the cliff. My heart pounding, I grasped the protruding shelves of rock and carefully moved ever higher.

I followed the undulating lines of the rock face for what seemed an eternity. There were false lips and a few openings much too small for a human body, but I could see larger openings above me.

I kept going, climbing carefully. I turned my head to look for my next handhold and felt a tug on my hair. I tried to pull my head away in order to see where my hair had gotten caught but my hair stayed taut, pulling painfully. I couldn't let go of my handhold, so I pulled my head away in spite of the pain and looked.

There was a stone face embedded in the cliff wall and it had gripped my hair in its mouth! My knees turned to water and I had to force myself to concentrate to keep my hold. I looked around wildly and saw more faces staring at me with stony eyes and open mouths.

I had to get away! I reached up for a higher handhold and heard the whoops of the Huntress and her Hunters behind me. Very close behind me! Arrows began to smack into the cliff walls around me.

Panicking, I grabbed for the first handhold I saw – and felt a stony mouth close on my fingers. I screamed and tried to pull my hand away but it was stuck fast. Still screaming, I scaled a bit higher, trying to regain my hand.

There was a sudden, sharp pain in my leg. I looked down to see an arrow embedded in the back of my thigh.

I woke up to find myself hanging by my hand still clamped in the stone face's mouth. Blood was seeping down my leg from the arrow wound. The Huntress and her Huntsmen were gone.

Scrabbling for a hold, expecting the rock-mouth to let go at any moment and send me down to my death, I hugged the cliff wall, careful to stay out of range of any more mouths. I tried to ignore the staring faces as I began working my fingers out of the mouth of the stone creature.

I lost some skin in the process but finally managed to free my hand.

I felt my way around the lip of a ledge, waving my right hand out in front of me like a blind person. At last my exploring fingers felt a large space just above me. I could make out a darkness deeper than the surface rock. If I crawled up, I would be on a ledge that was, I hoped, the location of a cave.

Praying that I wouldn't encounter any snakes – didn't I read somewhere that no snakes existed in Faerie? Or was that Ireland?? – I crawled over the lip onto the wide ledge. Before me was a deep depression in the rock.

It was large enough to hold me. I crawled in and curled up on the floor, knees drawn up under my cloak, and pulled the hood over my eyes. I was done. I didn't even have the strength to tend to the arrow. Dizzy and sick to my stomach, I lay on the cold stone floor and finally gave up.

Gildan walked toward the Steams as a rain shower dissolved into mist. There came a peal of thunder so loud it shook the ground, and he looked up to see not the bolt of lightning he expected, but The Huntress and her Huntsmen rising above the treetops. He dropped to the ground and covered his head with his arms. This was the ages-old signal to the Huntsmen that he surrendered to them.

As their war cries faded into the sky, he stood up and brushed off his robe. Suddenly the meaning of the sighting became clear to him – Odessa must not yet be dead. They must be chasing her somewhere in this vicinity!

The Huntsmen had come from the Eastern Steams. Gildan turned in that direction and started running. His long legs covered the distance quickly. Soon he entered an area between the lake and the Steams. It was dark, but his magical eyes allowed him to see. He was almost into the Steams when a rank smell assaulted his senses – it smelled like death. He slowed his pace and was so focused for movement around him that he almost tripped over the corpse.

The figure was much too large to be Odessa and it was clearly a male, lying on his side. Gildan was repulsed by the odor but rolled the dead man onto his back. He didn't at first recognize the man, but the smell was identification enough. He stood up and backed away, unconsciously rubbing his hand on his robe.

What is the Rotter doing here? Why did The Huntress kill him? Only Fae who betrayed her – and then Gildan noticed the dark stain on the ground at the feet of the body. There were no wounds to account for that blood. He searched the surrounding area and found a small splash of blood staining some pebbles a couple yards away from the body.

Someone had come this way who had been wounded but was not bleeding heavily. Whoever it was had gone into the Steams, into the same area Gildan had seen the Huntsmen leave. He moved quickly into the forest bordering the Steams. There was still a chance that she was alive.

The pain was relentless. It drilled into my leg like a wild thing desperate to escape from a trap. If I lay perfectly still, it was agony. If I moved even a little, the pain flared and my stomach threatened to erupt. I huddled into a little ball and wished for death.

Slowly, oh so slowly, my body began to adjust to the pain and relax a bit.

I didn't realize I was falling asleep until I caught myself dreaming. I heard my name called by a familiar voice, but couldn't place it. The calling began just at the edge of my hearing and slowly came closer. It was a good voice. It was someone I trusted. I couldn't think of his name, but I liked him. Even though I called back to the voice, it continued to cry out my name. "I'm here!" I shouted in the dream, "I'm here!"

Gildan sprinted across the meadow toward the cliffs he knew bordered a river far below. The mountainous outcropping held a few caves that would be large enough to provide a hiding place. He called Odessa's name repeatedly, but heard no answer.

He skirted the top of the cliffside at its lowest point and began walking the edge, calling her and looking for openings. There! A moan! He dropped to his knees and peered into a depression in the rock. There was a glimpse of pale flesh and another moan.

"Odessa! It is Gildan. Are you all right?"

She didn't answer in words, just moaned as if suffering intense pain. Gildan reached into the hole and pulled the hood away from her face. She was unconscious and moaning, her skin pale, drops of sweat running from her hairline. An arrow jutted from the back of her thigh and blood had pooled on the rock beside her leg.

He didn't dare move her. Working quickly, he tore a strip of cloth from her cloak and applied it as a tourniquet to her leg. Then, with a grimace, he yanked out the arrow. Odessa cried out but remained unconscious. Gildan used the tourniquet cloth to bind the wound and then dropped to sit at the cave opening.

What do I do? I dare not leave her. But what good will I be if The Huntress comes? The only way to escape her is to hold her off until dawn of the third day or …

He sat up straighter, struck by his next thought *…or leave Faerie! Why did I not think of this earlier? By the Gods, I can take her back to Earth and the Huntress cannot touch her.*

The Huntsmen's horn blew a monotone note. Odessa twitched and moaned at the sound. Her eyes opened.

I saw something moving at the opening to my cave of hiding. The horn, I had heard the horn, so this had to be – HER! I gave a frightened squeak and tried to press myself even smaller.

"Odessa?" the voice from my dream said my name once more. "It is Gildan."

The moon was shining down on the cliffside and I could see his white hair and the edges of his arms.

"Gildan … are you a ghost?" It was an effort just to speak. The pain was still nearly unbearable and each word threatened to make me vomit.

"Not yet," he replied. "Are you ill?"

"Yes. Migraine. Headache. Very sick."

"Can …walk? We have …time. The Horned …is com …"

"You're fading in and out. Can't hear."

Gildan felt fear slide through him. He leaned down and spoke softly into Odessa's ear. Then he dug beneath his robe to find the oak tree charm hanging from his neck. He pulled the charm off the chain and tucked it into the pocket of her cloak.

"Gildan?" she called, "Gildan, where did you go? Gildan?"

He kissed her forehead and crawled from the cave. He sat down on the ledge and began to call softly. After a few moments, the shadows moved and walking toward him was a tuxedo cat. It scrambled up to him and rubbed its cheek against his knee in greeting.

"Hello little one. I have a job for you." Gildan leaned down and whispered into the cat's ear.

Then he stood up, straightened his shoulders, and strode in the direction from which the horn had sounded. When he heard the sounds of hooves on rock, he changed shape and sprinted away from Odessa's hiding place.

With his physical shape a copy of Odessa, Gildan drew the Huntress and her hunters away toward the mountains that led to BacchusYard. This was an area he knew well, even in the dark. He had just entered a stand of alders that bordered the mountain itself when he heard panting behind him. A Hell-Wolf was gaining on him. He heard the bellows of the Huntsmen as they rode the air behind the wolf.

Gildan grinned. He gave it all he had, feeling the Hell-Wolf snapping at his cloak as it billowed behind him. Only yards ahead of the wolf, he ran straight into the wall of the mountain and melted into it. The Hell-Wolf was so close on his heels that it smacked muzzle-first into the rock wall.

Chapter 16
The Fairy Ring

When I woke up, the sun was shining outside my little cave. Groaning, I crawled out of the sheltering rock, stiff and sore and sick to my stomach. I tried to stand but my head swam and I vomited. The pain had lessened, a bit number now, but was still there.

These damned migraines are so unpredictable. Shouldn't this one have reversed what I can see? Why can I still see Faerie? Maybe they're just plain headaches here?

The sunlight hurt my eyes. I covered them with my hand and slumped to the ground.

I had dreamt that Gildan had found me in my hiding place and had told me how to be safe from the Huntress. I began to weep as a helpless anger swept through me. I pounded the ground with my fist and kicked my feet. I tried to scream, but that made my head hurt worse. When the pain overgrew my tantrum, I was reduced to writhing on the ground until I felt foolish.

That was when I noticed that the arrow was no longer in my leg and the wound had been bandaged. *How could that be? Had Gildan really been here? Why would he leave me if he had been here? But who else could have taken care of me?* I shivered. Had The Huntress done this just to keep me alive for another day?

I licked my dry lips. There was water in my bag; I opened it and withdrew the skin. After a long drink, I glanced at the cliff edge past my cave. I re-corked the skin and without really knowing why, walked to the edge.

The ground declined gradually toward an animal-made trail down the side of the hill. Below, intersecting the forest and the mountain, a river wound its way through the valley.

The river. Something about a river. Gildan had said something about a river in my dream. I looked down at it, feeling it pull on me. *Oh hell, why not? Where else do I have to go? Maybe following the river will take me to Bacchus Yard!*

The decline was steeper than it looked and my wound still hurt, so I sat on my behind and slid carefully down to the path. The view was incredible – mist rising from the river, glinting silver in the sunlight. *Maybe I can travel by river. Maybe I can find a boat!*

The trail took me down the cliffside into a pine forest. The clean scent of the trees comforted my aching head as I made my way on layers of fallen needles. I walked for a while and suddenly realized the pain had become bearable.

As I walked, something white gleamed amongst the trees ahead. It was small and moving toward me out of the forest. It began to run and I saw with disbelief that it was none other than my Milk

Monster, her white patches flashing in the filtered sunlight.

She reached me and began curling her body around my legs. I stroked her, murmuring, so happy to see something so familiar that my eyes started to water. I picked her up and loved on her for a moment before she leapt from my arms. She walked a few steps away and looked back at me and then walked a little farther and repeated the look back.

She wants me to go with her, I realized, so I walked after her. She led me back into the forest. Before long, we walked into a clearing and I stopped, dumbstruck. I was looking at an enormous mushroom. Its stalk was taller than I and I could fit easily under the bell-shaped cap. Delighted, feeling like Alice in Wonderland, I walked underneath and gazed up at the gills high above my head. This was like another dream!

Equally amazing was the sight of other mushrooms just like it. They formed a huge circle, some of the caps facing in different directions, but there was no mistaking the circular formation. I had found a real Fairy Ring!

Again, I felt a vague tug on my consciousness. Had Gildan told me about this, too? I couldn't quite remember. Milk Monster was sitting beside a smaller mushroom that squatted in the exact center of the circle. It was just like the mushrooms I had seen in some illustrations from *Alice in Wonderland*. It had a bright red cap with white dots and was just tall enough that I could sit on it. I just had to do that!

As I reached the mushroom, I realized that Milk Monster was gone. I peered behind the stalk of the cheery mushroom but she was nowhere to be seen.

"Stop right there, Human!"

I was startled – and then horror-struck – to see Adram striding toward me from the outer edge of the Fairy Ring opposite me. His dark eyes blazed, his usually pale skin was rosy and sweaty, and his hands glowed red-hot as they reached for me.

I definitely did not want to be touched by those hands – I knew they would burn me badly. I backed away.

There came a rush of wind, and then pine needles, dirt, and fragments of mushroom rose into the air between Adram and me. The vortex of the whirlwind became the figure of Tempestra. She pointed at Adram and the swirling wind slammed into him, pushing him backward.

Over her shoulder, Tempestra shot me a look. "Go to the middle of the circle!"

I obeyed and hurried to the red mushroom with white dots, the only one of its kind in the Ring.

"Tempestra, what in red blazes are you doing?" Adram yelled, pushing his way forward through the buffeting wind that surrounded only him.

Tempestra giggled. "I changed my mind. I want her to go home."

Adram struggled against the wind but made little progress. Tempestra watched, smirking as she blew kisses with one hand while holding him at bay with the other.

Sudden thunder shook the skies. We all looked up. Boiling, black clouds signaled what I feared – The Huntress had arrived. The hellacious hunting party broke through the cloud cover and set down in the meadow between the Ring and the forest.

I stood paralyzed beside the red and white mushroom. *This is it. I've lost. I'm going to die in Faerie after all.* My mind screamed for my frozen body to run, run, but my muscles were locked. I stood gasping for air through a choking throat.

The Huntress turned toward Tempestra, who dropped her arm; the windstorm died. Adram smirked at her as he crossed to stand beside one of the Hunters. Tempestra disappeared in a puff of wind.

A sudden thought jerked my gaze to the sinister figure of the Huntress. It's daytime! How can the Huntress even be here? As I stared, I realized that her form was shimmering, as though she was being forced to use a lot of her power just to keep her form. *No wonder I'm not dead. She can't hurt me when she's like this.*

There was movement at the forest's edge and Elves oozed out of the shadows to join the hunting party. My knees threatened to give way as I saw two of them drag Lull out of the forest and march her to the front of the group. The Huntress may not have the strength to hurt me, but the Elves surely could.

I had to try twice to get her name past my tight throat. "Lull, have they hurt you?"

Lull wrenched her arms out of the Elves' grasp and took a step away from them, toward me. "No, I'm all right."

"Why are you here? Is this your punishment? To watch me die?" I looked to the crowd of predators. "You've won. I can't escape. Hasn't she suffered enough? Let her go and I'll come to

176

you willingly." I hoped no one would point out that my position was hopeless whether they released Lull or not.

One of the Elves bent forward and said something to Lull that I couldn't hear, but it was obviously a command.

"Odessa, please come to me. Come away from there and let me hold you," Lull called out, reaching her arms toward me while simultaneously making tiny negative shakes of her head.

I remained where I was, trying to figure out what she was trying to tell me. Lull glanced at the Elves and the Huntress. "If you won't come to me, I'll come to you."

She took a step in my direction and no one stopped her. She walked slowly toward me. "Odessa, you know that I love you, don't you? You know I would never hurt you. You can trust me." Her voice shook as she continued, "You do trust me, don't you?"

"Of course I do," I replied. I was terribly confused. Lull looked rigid, as though expecting an arrow in the back.

"They want you to come away from that mushroom and come over to them. I'll walk with you."

She reached me and pulled me into a tight hug. She whispered, "I'm sending you home. I love you."

She shoved me and I fell backward onto the cap of the spotted mushroom. Thunder boomed as the air was displaced. My last glimpse of Faerie was the vision of Lull turning to face the enemy.

I woke up lying on the ground in my back yard. I blinked up at the familiar oak branches and blue sky. Dry, dead leaves skittered over my body in the fall breeze. The ground was cold and lumpy with roots. I sat up and saw the back door of my red and white house, the glass windows of my studio … home! *Ohmygod, home!*

Not quite able to believe it, afraid it was but a dream, I got to my feet and staggered weakly down the sidewalk to my door, knees wobbling and breath shaky. As I approached the porch, there was a rustle of leaves, and Milk Monster leaped from the tall grass and then strolled over to wind around my ankles, tail high, seeking attention.

I leaned down to pet her and was almost surprised to find she was real. We walked up the steps to the porch and then into the house. Milk Monster got underfoot, as she'd always done, nagging at me to hurry as I poured her milk – amazingly still fresh in the fridge – and scooped some crunchy cat food. She didn't seem to care that I was sobbing my heart out, as long as she got her milk. I really was home!

Chapter 17
Worlds Collide

The skies of Faerie reverberated as the Huntress screamed her rage. Her prey had escaped – and someone must pay! Circling above the clearing, she gestured for her Huntsmen to follow as she dug her heels into the sides of her Hell-Horse and forced it into a dive. As soon as their hooves touched land again, the Wild Hunt became a physical force.

The army of Elves began shooting quills and arrows at the Huntsmen. Using their horses as weapons, the Huntsmen trampled the Elves, ignoring the projectiles as brittle bone repelled the quills. The Hell-Wolves took down running Elves who were too panicked to fight back.

The Huntress shrieked and howled as she spilled Elven blood by horse and by arrow. Only when there were no more Elves standing did she stop shrieking and killing. Still unsatisfied, she reared her horse and whooped for her riders. The undead riders gathered and the Hell-Wolves dropped the limbs they were chewing – and all followed their leader back into the sky. There was a rumble of thunder and they were gone.

Within the Fairy Ring, safe from the melee, Lull crept out from beneath a sheltering mushroom. The horror of the bloody massacre met her eyes and she gasped.

Hearing footsteps behind her, she whirled to find Adram approaching. His entire body was glowing with fiery rage. Lull was frightened but stood her ground.

"Dare you raise a hand against the woman who tried to help you?" Lull challenged.

Adram snarled. "You have ruined everything, woman! Faerie will fall to the wrath of the Hunt-Goddess because of you. You raised me and now you have killed me. I owe you nothing!"

He reached for her and Lull ran. She dodged some bodies and leapt over others, running for the forest. She had almost made it when Adram grabbed her arm. She screamed as her flesh burned.

Adram snorted a laugh and reached for her neck. There was a dull sound of wood against skull and Adram fell unconscious to the ground, leaving Lull gasping and weeping and clutching her burned arm.

Gildan stepped out of the woods. "Good thing I held onto this stick," he said. He dropped it and took Lull into his arms, eyeing her scalded skin. "We must get this tended."

I sat curled up in my favorite old denim chair and paused in my writing. *What was that noise? Was it thunder?*

I'm keeping my promise to Gildan. How better to reach a wide audience than to write this book about my experiences and Faerie's and Earth's mutual decline? I'm hoping that the telling will be therapeutic as I progress.

My days at home so far have been a nightmare. I thought at first that being back in the comfort of my own home would lessen the emotional trauma of my time in Faerie, but I was wrong. I don't sleep well and I wake up screaming more often than not. I jump at every little noise. I keep seeing movement in my peripheral vision that turns out to be only my jagged nerves and imagination.

What will happen when I have my next migraine? Will it be normal or Fairy-producing? I have no way of knowing and the suspense is awful. It's just one more thing nagging at me.

The only small comfort I've found is the silver oak tree charm that Gildan must have slipped to me the last time I saw him. I was throwing away the dress and cloak that I had worn in Faerie when I found his silver charm.

Upon returning home, one of the first things I did was rip that clothing off. It stayed crumpled on the bathroom floor, making my stomach lurch every time I saw the dress and cloak. It took me two days before I could touch the wretched garments.

As I wadded up the cloak to dispose of it, I felt something hard, and discovered the oak tree charm in a pocket. Now I wear it on a silver chain around my neck. This I want to keep. Memories of Gildan are good ones, even though part of me very much fears seeing him again. I both long for and also dread ever seeing Gildan – or even Pillyswiggin or Gollysnuffle. It's not really Gildan that I fear, I guess, but what he represents. If I can see him, I can see Her.

It's Lull that I miss the most. She was the one who made my time in Faerie enjoyable and even fun. She was companion, mother-figure, and protector, all in one good-natured, fleshy and friendly half-woman. I feel great guilt that she sacrificed herself for me, and I will always grieve her loss. There is just no way she could have possibly remained standing against the wrath of the Huntress and her horde.

Part of me insists, though, that she's still alive, tending to her horses and chickens and baking nut loaves in her cheery kitchen. I'm sure that's just wishful thinking spawned from my guilt, but I can't help believing it.

As for the Huntress, I can't even imagine the outcome of what was happening when I left. I've done a little research and have discovered that the best way to escape her is to change worldly planes, which I have done, but even that is not guaranteed. One of my worst nightmares is that I'm struck by a migraine and I see her and the Huntsmen descending from the sky to my front yard. I still cringe every time I think I hear thunder.

I am so torn about Faerie! I want so badly to see Gildan again and learn of Lull's fate, but to return there is to ensure my own death. My only option to see Gildan again is to have one of "those" migraines and see Gildan here again. But then if I can see him, would I also see Her – is she also able to travel between worlds?

I loved living the simple life that Lull and I shared at her farm. I do so wish we could have continued that way. I hate this conflict within me. I love parts of Faerie and fear many others. I want so badly to return, but would I live out my life there? I don't know.

When I'm not writing this book, I'm working on a clay sculpture of Lull. I don't really need her likeness to remind me of her – I'll never forget her. I just want a bit of her around.

My writing was once again interrupted by an odd noise. This definitely wasn't thunder but something hitting the roof. The sound repeated itself in succession.

It's hail. Big hail. Must be a thunderstorm nearby.

I laid my notebook aside and went to the window. The world outside was sunny, the sky clear. Frowning, I turned away, only to hear another round of the mysterious thuds.

Acorns. It must be acorns.

I turned back to the window. There was no evidence of wind. None. I was used to the occasional acorn hitting the roof, but it took a strong wind to dislodge a bunch of them at once.

Besides, it's the wrong time of year.

I walked to the front door, opened it, and looked out. The neighborhood was quiet. There was no one around, much less anyone throwing things onto my roof. I walked out into the front yard, looking around, intending to check the back yard, and then I happened to glance up.

Ohmygod! Arrows!

The roof was studded with arrows. As I stood there gaping, unable to believe what I was seeing, two Hell-Wolves sailed over the roof from the back of the house and dove toward me. I screamed, backing away, and tripped over my own feet.

The Hell-Wolves landed right beside me – and immediately became discarnate on the ground. They snarled and snapped viciously but were unable to touch me in their non-physical state.

I scrambled to my feet and raced into the house, slamming and locking the front door behind me. In panic I went from room to room, searching for something but not knowing what I was looking for. A weapon? A place to hide? Gildan?

I had heard thunder earlier. It was either very far away or the sound of the Hell-Wolves breaking into this world. The Huntress couldn't be far behind.

"Goddammit, Gildan, I need you!" I screamed to the empty house, knowing that even if he did arrive I wouldn't be able to see or hear him.

Thinking of Gildan made me pause in my search.

I'm panicking just the same way I did at the start of the Wild Hunt. I have to calm down and think clearly. That would be the first thing Gildan would say to me if he were here.

I forced myself to take deep breaths until I felt in better control of myself. Then I walked instead of running to the kitchen to find a weapon. The best I could find was a knife, but that would be useless against archers.

My best bet is to stay in the house. At least I'm safe from arrows in here.

I turned to put the knife away – and screamed. The pale-dead leering face of a Huntsman was staring at me through the kitchen window! He was floating in the air, bobbing like a cork in water. He thrust a rotting tongue toward me and made licking motions.

"Go away! Leave me alone!" I shrieked.

I lunged toward the window, knife raised. The Huntsman flinched, not expecting my reaction, and put out a hand to steady himself. He touched the glass and turned to spirit.

I yanked the curtain closed and then did the same with all the curtains in the house.

Oh, God, Gildan, what do I do? If only I could see you, talk to you. I'd give anything – wait! Maybe I can see him if I have another migraine. It's worth a try.

I flung open the refrigerator door and pulled out all the trigger foods inside – chocolate, cheese, pickles. Normally I could eat these things in small quantities without inducing a migraine, but only if I never had them in combination or in large amounts.

I tore open the packages and gagged the foods down. All the while, I expected the Huntress and her horde to come smashing through my windows and doors.

I stopped eating in mid-pickle.

Wait a minute. The Hell-Wolves had become non-physical when they touched the ground, and the Huntsman, too, when he had touched the house. That means they can't leave the air! As long as I stay inside they can't hurt me.

I finished the pickle and chased it with a last piece of chocolate. Then I paced the confines of the house, checking the safety of each room and reassuring myself that I was safe inside the house. I was exhausted but couldn't sit still. I kept anticipating the onset of the migraine, willing it to come, and the tension made me even more anxious.

A yowl pierced the air out front.

I know that yowl!

I ran to the living room window and peeked through a gap in the curtains. Milk Monster was in the front yard, her back arched and fur standing on end to make herself look bigger than she was. As I watched, one of the Hell-Wolves dove at her, coming within inches of the small spitting cat. Monster stood on her haunches and whipped out a clawed paw, swiping the face of the Hell-Wolf as it passed over her head. Had it been another inch closer, she would have been snatched up in its jaws.

I opened the front door.

"Monster! Come here, baby! Come to the house!"

She recognized my voice and looked my way. She dropped to all fours, scanned the sky for danger, and then started running toward me and safety.

Thwap! The small black-and-white cat kept bounding for a few steps before she fell, an arrow piercing her torso. She twitched a couple times and then lay still.

I lost my mind. Oblivious to the danger, consumed with utter rage, I ran out into the front yard and scooped up my lifeless, precious friend. I screamed at the sky, choking on tears.

"You bitch! She was just a kitty!" I hugged Milk Monster to my chest. "You win, you awful bitch! Come and get me. I just don't care anymore!"

I stared up at the sky, and realized that the migraine had started. The oh-so-familiar colorless kaleidoscope was blocking part of my vision.

Too late, too late.

There was a deafening boom of thunder, and the Huntress materialized in the sky. Her fire-eyed horse reared, then swooped toward me. The horde followed, including the Hell-Wolves.

I stood watching them, trying to blink away the blurred and moving obstruction to my vision. I glanced behind me but there was no sign of Gildan coming to my rescue.

The Huntress reined her horse to a stop high above the driveway. She threw back the hood of her cloak and I found myself staring at a skull with glowing yellow eyes. Wisps of long, dark hair clung to parts of the skull. The crescent moon tiara on its bony pate would have been funny had it not been so completely terrifying.

My knees went weak, threatening to give way beneath me. I dropped Milk Monster, all the strength in my body fighting my unsteady knees. I was panic-stricken but also resigned to the fact that I just couldn't win against a hunter-goddess.

This is it. I'm going to die. But I'm going to die fighting!

As the Huntress reached into her quiver for an arrow, I pulled the arrow out of Milk Monster's body and charged toward the Huntress.

Barely two steps toward her, I felt someone behind me grab my shoulders and propel me beneath a nearby oak tree. I tried to see who had accosted me but I was being held against the trunk of the tree and the side of my face was pressed against the rough bark.

"Now," said a male voice, loud to my ear.

The Huntress laughed, a horrifying sound between a hiss and a cackle, and aimed her weapon at me and Gildan.

He's come to the rescue but only to die at the hands of the Huntress.

"Gildan, I …"

I was interrupted by the laughter of the Huntress suddenly turning to shrieks of pain and surprise. Around her, the Huntsmen were also screaming and flailing, their horses bucking and kicking. The Hell-Wolves were convulsing and howling.

Gildan let me go and I saw the Elementals, Poseida and Tempestra, standing together before the Huntress and her horde. They were gesturing with graceful commands and the elements were following their directions.

A fierce ice storm had erupted just above the Huntress and her minions. Large, sharp daggers of ice, propelled by a howling wind, were flaying the flesh off the undead bones. Although Gildan and I were sheltered by the covering of the oak branches, some of the sleet stung my face in hot pinpricks.

Sharp chunks of huge hail followed the ice, shattering bones and skulls. The hail was also breaking branches; some crashed to the ground around us, followed by twigs and slivers of dead leaves and other debris caught up in the strong wind.

One by one, the horde were torn to pieces, falling from the sky in a rain of broken bones and dead flesh. The pieces hit the ground, turned to spirit, and were dispersed by the whipping wind.

The Huntress fell from her horse as its broken body collapsed to the ground. She landed beside it and both were dissolved and blown away by the wind. Within minutes there was no trace of either the Huntress or her horde.

Tempestra jumped up and down with delight, once again resembling a high school cheerleader.

"We did it, Poseida!" she squealed, impulsively embracing Poseida.

The ever-regal Poseida endured the hug with a half-smile, then pulled away and smoothed her dress. "We did indeed."

Poseida looked to Gildan. "We should have merged our forces long ago and rid Faerie of that awful predator before so many Folk were lost. Thank you, sir, for insisting that we do this."

Gildan smiled at her. "To tell the truth, I had run out of ideas. There was no recourse but to try a last resort."

He turned to me. I was still standing under the oak, staring at the spot where the Huntress had dissolved.

"Odessa? Are you all right?"

My answer was to fall flat on my face.

Epilogue

I have kept my promise to Gildan. The book you are holding is evidence of that. I hope that humanity will stop the destruction of their planet for their own sake as well as that of Faerie. There are consequences to all that we do in both realms. I hope this book is a beneficial consequence of my time in Faerie.

You cannot imagine the joy I felt when Gildan told me that Lull was alive and well. He took me to see her and we spent a few days together before I came back home to finish this book. She told me that Adram had been stripped of his membership in the Silver Company and had been banished to the Darklands.

Writing *Suddenly Fairies* did turn out to be therapeutic, and it helped me to make the hardest, yet easiest decision of my life. Faerie is not the utopian land filled with Flower Fairies sipping nectar all day that I had thought it was not all that long ago. Although the Huntress and her Huntsmen are gone, there are still challenges to be faced.

I've learned that darkness and beauty co-exist in both worlds. To me, the terror of the Wild Hunt is now overshadowed by the peace and contentment I found living with Lull on her farm. The heart wants what the heart wants, and my heart wants Faerie.

By the time you read this, I will have left this realm again to live in Faerie. I know that I've made the right decision. How? Because a few days ago, while standing in Lull's yard discussing whether or not I should follow my heart, a tiny tuxedo kitten ran into the yard and seemed to recognize me. She walked right past Lull, with her tiny tail held high, and wound around my legs, mewing. And that was that.

www.ingramcontent.com/pod-product-compliance
Lightning Source LLC
Chambersburg PA
CBHW060645260626
47161CB00008B/3000